FEB   2019

3 WOMEN
4 TOWNS
5 BODIES

& other stories

TOWNSEND WALKER

Deeds Publishing | Atlanta

Published by Deeds Publishing in Atlanta, GA
www.deedspublishing.com

Printed in The United States of America

Cover design and text layout by Mark Babcock

Library of Congress Cataloging-in-Publications data is available upon request.

ISBN 978-1-947309-21-0

Books are available in quantity for promotional or premium use. For information, email info@deedspublishing.com.

First Edition, 2018

10 9 8 7 6 5 4 3 2 1

For Stormy

Contents

3 Women, 4 Towns, 5 Bodies

Francesca
London, Late 1990s

Our intro was *I'm A Woman*, though we barely were. Soft pink lights tracked us as we strutted across the stage. We stopped, leaned out to the audience, the top of our breasts on display. We pulled the pins from up-swept hair, swished the glossy black strands back and forth, then stood tall and proud. Ready to perform. Four men in dark suits, cuff links flashing, looked up. They were a cut above our usual Pink Flamingo clientele, they were.

Minutes earlier, Percy showed them to the front, fussed over seating them, broke out a bottle of his 25-year-old Scotch, and then hurried backstage, perspiration dripping off his face.

"I need for you and Lucia do your best. The one on the left is Sir George Bagot. This is big time."

I didn't know who he was then. Later, I found out he

was chairman of a big construction company and close to the new PM. Bagot stood out from the others, tall, long thin cheeks, wide red lips, blond hair combed tight to the head.

Lucia and I bit the ends of our long gloves to loosen them and peeled them down our arms. We turned around, undulated the length of our bodies and inch by inch our dresses slid down our backs, bums, and legs. The satin puddled on the floor, leaving two girls in black heels, black stockings, and pale bare cheeks. We swayed side to side, thrust our bottoms toward the men, danced with mincing steps that shook our bodies, bent over, heads between our knees, and winked.

Two chairs were brought out, *Black Magic Woman* with its organ intro came on. We made love to those chairs, to the men, trembling as we ground and thrust our pelvises quickly, rabidly, sinking into the seats, arms dangling. We leaned forward, eyes searching theirs, so they could see us breathless from the climax. They gasped, licked their lips, and raised their glasses.

Next, we kicked one leg over the back of the chair, slid the stockings off, stretched out the other leg, and peeled the nylons down. Stood, faced the men, bent down, showed them breasts begging to escape from the corsets, coddled our melons and caressed our inner thighs. I licked my lips and stared into Bagot's narrowed blue eyes. He was hungry. We unsnapped the corsets and faced the whistling men in lacy bras and G-strings. The lights went down, the small room now black. The men shouted.

Stripper, screaming slide trombone and drums, filled the room. Lights up, we toyed with our bra straps, pulled one down our shoulder, halfway up, then down further, uncovered more flesh, hugged our breasts, unhooked the bras, let it slip just to the top of our nipples. We cupped our breasts, offered them. Finally, dropped the lace, showed everything. Then we lowered ourselves to the floor and prowled on hands and knees, back and forth at the front of the stage, hips and tits swaying, daring the men to reach out and touch, moving into their grasp when they did.

We pulled out every stop, went beyond where we usually go, or let the customer go. Bagot and his friends must have thought so too, judging by the wads of fifty pound notes they stuffed in our G-strings.

* * *

Lucia and I met when we were five at the Convent San Zaccaria. I arrived first. My mother had run off with an Englishman in Venice on holiday. My father dumped me on the Benedictine nuns. Said he couldn't handle me. Abandoned twice, I was. Lucia arrived pale, gangly, and not friendly. Her parents died in a crash on the autostrada and her nonna claimed she couldn't raise a young child. Never tried, Lucia said. The nuns were happy. Besides being paid, they reckoned we were possibles for the habit, black robes to the ground, a white wimple and black veil. They were often delusional.

The first summer Sister Catrina took ten of us to the sea, bright swim-suited chicks on the beach. "Stay close girls, it's too deep for you and you never know what's out there."

But, Lucia and I swam out fifty meters, way over our heads, dove and picked up shells from the bottom. Our daring got us paddled when we came back. From then and forever we were best friends, willing to find more ways to break the rules.

In convent school, I got high marks in math and science. Lucia was a disaster, but she loved literature, the Goldoni plays where characters manipulate one another. The banter she picked up, her ability to drop into the role of the penitent, the proper lady, or the scold at a moment's notice got us out of some nasty fixes. We'd been out, met some boys, were caught by the nuns coming in the canal entrance after hours. Lucia lowered her eyes, acted frightened, "Oh Sister, we thought we heard a rat inside on the stairs, we shooed it away." Pointing to the ebbing water, "Look, there it is, swimming."

* * *

When I turned fourteen, Sister said my mother was in the reception room waiting to see me. I opened the door a crack. The room was quite formal with a green stone floor partly covered with oriental rugs, frescoed ceilings thirty feet high, and mirrored walls. In the corner, there was the twisted reflection of a woman and florid brush-mustachioed man sitting in tall gilt chairs. The woman who had abandoned me years earlier. Not at all the way I remembered her, heavier she was, in a dreadful lime green dress. I guessed the man was David, the one who'd taken her away. I stood outside watching. They looked around, squirmed in the narrow chairs, whispered to one another, gazed up at the ceiling.

When I walked into the room, the first thing she said, "Darling, I want you to come back to England with us."

"Why should I?" She hadn't even said hello.

"Your father has stopped paying the convent. I won't pay when I can give you a perfectly good education in London."

"I have a good one here, with the Sisters, thank you."

"In Italy, I don't think so."

"Well, I won't go."

"Really, darling, you don't have a choice." She'd gotten so English sounding.

I told her. "Not if I can't bring Lucia."

"Who is this Lucia?" My mother said.

"My one and only best friend."

She sputtered and talked about the size of their flat

in London and the expense of two girls. "It is totally impossible, Francesca. I cannot agree."

"Alright then, I'll stay here," stood up and stomped toward the door.

Lucia came into the room, took my hand, walked up to my mother and curtsied. "Madam, I have heard so many lovely things about you. It is a great pleasure meeting you in person."

"And you are?"

"Lucia Chiara Monti. Francesca is my best friend in the world."

David's mouth fell open. Both of us were tall, Lucia more than me. And she had filled out faster. She'd arranged her long black hair over her left shoulder and her blouse was near unbuttoned beneath her uniform jacket.

David stuttered, but finally got some words out. "Dearest, if our Francesca is set on bringing her friend, we'll certainly find a way to make do. Such a well-mannered, cultured child." Not precisely his thoughts. Once back in England, when everyone else was out, he backed her into a wall and started to grope her. A well-placed knee sent him off.

It was a mean little apartment that Mama and David had, small, dark. Lucia and I had to share a single bed in a small room cluttered with three patterns of floral wallpaper, pinks, browns, and blues. Ghastly. The convent in Venice was a palace by comparison, built for daughters of the nobility. Legends of the ladies who lived there in the eighteenth century, at times with their lovers, fueled our imaginations...

When Lucia and I were about to turn seventeen, we were walking around Soho one afternoon after school, down Beak Street, saw a sign "Models Wanted." Lucia opened the door of the Pink Flamingo and dragged me in with her. Models, not exactly. Show girls, girls that showed what they had, that's what they wanted, and both of us had something worth seeing. Percy promised us gobs of money just to dance and take our clothes off. And we wanted to be able to buy frocks down on Kings Road. Wasn't happening with the allowance we got from David.

* * *

Sir George had his fingers in many money pots. He'd inherited and, he had been particularly clever in the market. Potassium, that's the one I think he cornered. He took a fancy to me and always included Lucia for one of his friends. That meant dinners at nice restaurants where the staff fawned over him. Such respect for a title. My favorite spot was Kettners, where Georgie reserved a small private room with a high green velvet booth and a small sitting area where we had champagne before tucking into their amazing steaks and triple fried chips. After, it was back to his flat in Chelsea, one he said his wife knew nothing about. On school nights we were back to Mum and David's flat before midnight, on weekends, next morning. In addition to being wined and dined we were generously assured we didn't have to wear the same frock twice.

Mama and David raised hell and kept threatening to toss us. But because the money we contributed (from our clerking jobs at Marks and Sparks, of course) and Georgie was Sir George, they were a bit tolerant. The more so because David's investment business hit a rough patch and his big investors took their cash, what was left, elsewhere. Pity. When David's firm was making money, he brought his young worker bees for dinner. Hot, some of them. David didn't like talking about the fish and chips of his work, but his lads did, so I found out a bundle about stocks and bonds. Like how to make money selling a stock you don't own. Rather fancied that's what I'd like to do. Make monster bets with other people's cash. Lucia's ideas ran to finding a rich widower. Neither of us was going to be poor.

* * *

One weekend Georgie invited Lucia and me down to Claven, his house in the country, if that's the term for a manor with a hundred rooms on 400 acres. A 48-hour pool party that didn't stop. People laid about where and with whom they fancied. After our first swim, I don't remember we wore much of anything until the time to take the train back to London. Percy wasn't happy, both of us gone the weekend, his busiest time, but for Sir George, so . . . Lucia and I came back totally knackered, skipped school and work on Monday and Tuesday. Mama hollered at us for sleeping in and smelling of booze.

"Sod off," I yelled back.

"It's been a year now. You two are a disgrace. Drinking and whoring. I blame it on that convent. Me and David can't undo what those nuns did to you. If I had known. But now, I've had it. Get out. Go."

We rented a small, but much nicer flat in Knightsbridge, behind Harrods on Hans Road. What with the money from the Pink Flamingo and Georgie's help, we did alright, we did, for seventeen. Bagged boring old Holland Park School. We were old enough, law didn't say we had to go.

* * *

Some two months on, Georgie invited Lucia and me down to Claven again. The only other guest was Douglas Thomson, Secretary of State for Defence. Georgie told me he had a weakness for very young, dark-haired girls. Lucia wore her school uniform, no make-up and hair in a ponytail. When I saw Thomson, I thought German Shepherd—smart, close cut mixed-color beard, dark brown darty eyes, man who gets his way. Just the four of us, with masses of servants. We sat around the pool, Georgie and Doug talked about the construction of an air base outside of Cairo. Royal Air Force would share it with the Egyptians. There were three other companies bidding on the project, and Georgie went on about how his firm, Horus, bested all. Lucia and I lounged beside them with our noses in Vogue and Bazaar. But, I like finance, so listened in. From what I could gather, they spent most of the time figuring out how they could make a few bob personally from the project.

We left the pool as clouds began to move in. I went up to Georgie's rooms; Lucia took Doug's arm to his. Late coming down to dinner, they were. Listening to Georgie and Doug by the pool and at dinner, I piped up, "I'm not sure I understand about sea shells and air-ports."

Georgie laughed, "Nothing to it, shells are companies without anything in them. More like pipes that let money flow from one place to another without anyone knowing where it ends up."

"Somebody has to know, don't they?"

"Shell is a better word than pipe. Not so terribly obvious. And there are more names to choose from, like baby's ear, beaded periwinkle, and angel. Like you."

"Thank you." I fluttered my eyes and bowed, acknowledging the compliment.

"And the more shells on the beach, the better."

After, the men did their port and cigar routine and chatted. Thomson discounted his chances as the next PM, but was keen to start a foundation promoting peace, where he'd be an intermediary in nasty situations in the Middle East. "Need a few quid for start-up and to keep it going," he said.

The conversation rather drifted to this and that. Georgie and Doug winked at one another, something they'd thought up, they swung around us, hoisted us up on the table and shouted, "Dance girlies, dance." And we did until they grabbed us down and chased us upstairs.

* * *

The following Wednesday, the Ministry of Defence announced the two billion pound air base contract was awarded to Horus Construction LTD. Ten days later, the London dailies headlined: Collusion between Secretary of State and Contractor? What Did Thomson and Bagot Talk About at Claven? One of Georgie's servants had talked to the *Daily Mail*. No details, but the servant had heard them talking about the air base several times over the course of the weekend. The propriety of the Secretary of State accepting the hospitality of a bidder the week before the announcement was somewhat questionable. The source also offered innuendoes about what might have taken place between two fifty-something married men of standing and two unnamed teenage girls.

In Parliament, Doug asserted the four bids for the project had been scrupulously analyzed by the Ministry and the Horus bid was superior in terms of construction experience, involvement of local contractors, and lower in price than the other bidders.

On the question of the young females seen with them at the manor, the newspapers said Doug claimed they were friends of the Bagot family visiting from Venice. One of their mothers was due to be with them, but fell ill at the last moment. "The mother insisted the girls take advantage of the weekend and Sir George and I felt obliged to show them a bit of the English countryside."

A week after the questions in Parliament, the *Independent* had another story on the airfield. "Secretary of State Rejects Ministry's Analysis." The newspaper cited a background paper that said the contract should have been awarded to Morgan Sindall because they had more experience in major projects and their bid was lower. Another round of questions for Doug, but he survived. Friends in high places.

Lucia and I continued at the Pink Flamingo, but became nervous to be seen around. We didn't want to get tagged as part of this affair. Nothing good could come of it. My Georgie dropped off the face. No calls from him and no responses when I called. It looked like our life of luxury might had come to a rude end. But more pressing, without Georgie, how would we pay the rent on the flat? Lucia had the answer. "Drop a bomb."

I did. He rang back five minutes later, whispering into the phone, "You're preggers?"

"No, Georgie darling, but now that I have your attention. Since the news broke you've been frightfully difficult to reach."

"Then why did you call?"

"I missed you, lovey."

"And I missed you, too. Now, why?"

"The Prime Minister's office rang up today, a Mr. Simpson he said his name was. They want to ask me questions about your project in Egypt."

"Darling Francesca, don't worry, you know nothing. Run down and talk to them and say you haven't a clue."

"But didn't you knock together Aten Assurance to protect the Ministry of Defence and Egyptian government from cost overruns?" I asked.

"Nothing new there, all public knowledge, my dear."

"But this probably isn't." I spoke as if I were reading a script for the first time. "Aten will enter into a zero-coupon swap with Barclay Bank. In five years, it will be worth 300 million pounds. After claims, isn't this where the shells come in?"

"Goddammit girl, you're in the wrong business."

"Half of what remains will be paid to Angel Wing Trust-Cayman, who will in turn pay it to Periwinkle Trust-Brunei. Secretary Thomson is the sole owner. The other half will be paid to Coquina Trust-St. Kitts which you own through Montrose & Company-Reno. Only there won't be claims?"

"This is a legitimate business transaction. How can you think otherwise?"

"If I've got this right, only Secretary of State for Defence Thomson can approve claims."

"Are you accusing him of betraying his position in the government?"

"I forgot one detail. That swap structure on the premium grosses up the insurance amount to meet MOD requirements, but the full amount will be realized only at the end of five years, do I have that right?"

"How did a bimbo like you ever learn about swaps? Bloody hell!"

"I found this little book by an American banker, Walker I think his name is, explained everything, like swaps, options, and all sorts of derivatives.

"What do you want?" Shouting now, he was.

"I like Swiss accounts. A girl can dream, can't she?"

"I expect you to use the three million pounds you find in those accounts to leave London. The entire British Isles, for that matter."

"Ta, Ta, ducky. Will I see you again?"

"Not likely. Wherever you go, be sure to take Lucia with you."

Gianni
Bologna, 2009

A cold gray October day. Gloom crowded the room, turning my office into a cemetery, a burial ground of deadbeat clients. My bank account was bleeding, my suit worn as a mortician's smile. Emilio, the barman at the corner café, left an Aperol Spritzer on a table for me in the evening, like leaving a saucer of cream for a stray cat.

Late in the afternoon, a delicate silhouette appeared behind the frosted glass. The knob turned, the door creaked, and in she walked. My nonna told me, "There are two kinds of trouble in this world, the kind to run from and the kind to embrace." Grazie nonna, but how do I tell the difference?

The woman's eyes were obsidian, but warm, very warm.

"I am Signora Fuoco, Lucia Fuoco."

My gaze moved down her legs. It took a while, to her bloody feet clad in delicate gold sandals.

"What? What is this? . . .Please sit." I pushed a chair toward her.

I went to the WC, found a basin, filled it with warm water, took a bar of soap and a towel. I knelt, unclasped the sandal, and placed her fragile foot in my hand. It floated there as I cleaned her long thin toes. Then the other foot, carefully, gently removing all traces of blood.

"Thank you, Signor Nero. I cannot stay long, but I need to know there is someone who will help me."

"Yes, of course I will. What can I do?" Looking up, I saw a face sorrow had profaned.

"Giancarlo is dead."

"Who?"

"My lover." Her lips trembled.

"When did it happen?"

"An hour ago."

"Where?"

"Hotel Al Cappello Rosso."

"Did you call the police?"

"No, oh no. I couldn't."

She'd met Giancarlo at his pasta shop, Il Pastificio Gustare. "My husband fancies himself a gourmet, so I became a loyal customer."

One of the most famous pasta makers in Italy, Gustare had made a surprising rise for a boy from Palermo. Surprising, because northerners are suspicious of anyone hailing from south of Rome, even more than those from the Eternal City itself.

"Every day I went to the shop and everyday Giancarlo and I talked. We talked about things more and more personal, things close to the heart. One day he invited me to coffee. Two days later we were lovers." She paused. Her eyes sparkled and her voice dropped to a whisper. "We had three months of happiness. O Madonna, such bliss."

Her composure crumbled as tears flooded her face. I sat, waiting. She took a handkerchief from her purse. Haltingly, continued. "Today was our first time together for a week. I'd been in Venice visiting my nonna."

She rose from her chair, a sinuous wraith.

"I must get back home now." Her eyes, not blinking, pulled me in. "You will help me?"

"Of course, I will."

Did I have a choice?

* * *

The next morning, no trace of yesterday's frightened woman. Dames. Yesterday, a doe. Today, a tigress. She dropped an envelope on the desk.

"Ten thousand euros, plus another three thousand to buy a new suit. You can't go about in those clothes."

True, my suit was as threadbare as the carpet under my feet. But then most of my cases called for nights in bars buying for losers with loose lips.

"Tell me the name of the person that killed Giancarlo, give me proof and I'll give you another ten thousand euros."

The struggle to suppress my joy about so much cash must have emerged as a frown. Her face wrinkled with concern. "I trust you're comfortable with the arrangement?"

I was puzzled. Why did Giancarlo matter so much?

She answered my unspoken question. "I want to see justice done. He was a good man."

Unlikely, but not the time to probe.

"Signora, did you always meet at the same hotel?"

"He knows," her voice quavered, "*Knew* the manager. Our room had a private entrance."

"This morning I couldn't find anything in the news-papers about him or anyone else dying in the city. You're sure?"

"We took a nap after we made love." Her eyes closed in reverie and a beatific smile crossed her lips. "Then I took a bath. When I came back into the room…"

She put her hands over her eyes as if they would block the vision in her head.

"Too horrible. He was gone and blood everywhere."

She melted in the chair. I might have put my arms around her, but stayed put, finding some non-existent lint to pick off my sleeve, hoping my face didn't betray my thoughts.

She bit hard on her lower lip, trying not to cry. "How will I be able to go on without him? He is the first man who understood me."

* * *

Ten thousand euros into the account and then to the best men's store in town. Though every man is as heaven made him, Ermenegildo Zegna did me proud. And with a visit to the barber, a different Gianni Nero strode the streets of Bologna.

I went back to the office and called my friend Nico in the police department. No bodies. Nico knew I wouldn't tell him why I was asking, so didn't waste time on the question. Over to Al Cappello Rosso. The hotel was in an ochre colored palazzo that had been a favorite of cardinals since the 14th century, hence the name. In its current incarnation, the hotel had lost some of its sanctity, or perhaps not. I made discrete inquiries of the bellman, slipped him a 100 euro note and learned nothing, but he provided a key. I went around to the back, found the narrow cobblestoned lane leading to the private entrance, walked up two flights, and introduced myself into the room. Its oval shape created an embrace, sun warmed a simple white bed, ceiling frescos of gamboling gods and goddesses in pinks and pale blues about to break a commandment, seven came to mind. But, no sign of blood. Who in the hotel was working with the killers? How did the killer get in the room? The same way I did? 100 euros to the bellman?

Back down on the street, footsteps behind me and

a mumbled "Mind your own business." A sharp rap on the back of the head and my knees hit the cobblestones. Then, a couple of kicks to the ribs. Some stronzo tried to ruin my new suit or stop the investigation. I'd be willing to let them if only the lady, and the money, weren't so delicious. Too many coincidences at this hotel. Someone was told I was there.

I got myself bandaged at Soc. Coop. Sociale, threw down a stiff scotch at del Sole, then walked by Signor Fuoco's bank. I had no doubt he had arranged Gustare's murder. But how did the banker find out about the affair, and who did the job for him. Maybe the two thugs who rapped me on the head. The bank was a 16th century sandstone building at the end of Piazza Maggiore. A driver was washing a long black Lancia with the bank's crest on the door. He was a lean wrinkled man with a droopy eye and sullen air, though a smart gray uniform gave him a bit of class. It took a few minutes of patter about soccer and Bologna FC for Massimo to turn talkative. I told him I worked for potential investors in the bank. According to Massimo, Signor Fuoco was a man who knew his business and allowed no one to be careless or dishonest with him. Even long time employees had been sacked for the smallest infraction. Massimo picked him up every day at 8:45, from 1:30 to 3:00 he had lunch with customers, home at 8:15. The driver was on call if the Fuocos went out at night.

"With the new signora, he goes to the theatre more

often. They met there some years ago. After I took her home the first night, they were never apart. She made sure of it."

He put his finger to the side of his nose. "No woman can change a fool into a wise man, but any woman can change a wise man into a fool."

* * *

The sun was setting, Signora Fuoco strode into my office clad in a flared skirt, diagonal cut azure jacket, black hair tumbling off her right shoulder. She reached out, took my hands, then touched the bandage. A cloud of roses and jasmine enveloped me.

"Oh Gianni, because of me?"

My expression, somewhere between it's nothing, and please-touch-me-again. "Some alleys are darker than others," I rasped. So now I needed more information. "Yesterday, we were telling me about how you met your husband."

"My parents died when I was five. Nonna placed me in a convent in Venice. Ten years ago, when I turned eighteen she sat me down and told me that she'd arranged for me to marry Signor Luigi Fuoco. 'A kind man, though a little older. He will take care of you and give you a respectable life.'" Lucia finished the recitation with her hands folded in her lap and feet together, a convent girl.

"I had no choice, without money or training in anything practical. He gives me a generous allowance and has provided for me in the event anything happens to him."

She paused and turned away, wistfully. A tale recounted with such piety. Brava! Should I believe the chauffeur? They met at the opera. Or her?

"Signora, is there any way your husband could have discovered your relationship with Giancarlo? Something you might have done, a new gesture, a sound, anything that you did differently when you two were alone?"

She flushed, turned away and got up. "Tomorrow," she said softly. "I can only be gone for a few moments now."

I held the door for her. She brushed my cheek with her fingers.

"You are handsome in your new clothes. Ciao, Signor Gianni Nero."

* * *

I had two different stories about Lucia and I was only two days into the investigation. I called a pal in Venice and asked him to check out the Convent San Zaccaria. When was she there? When did she leave? Why? Then, the society columnist at *Il Resto del Carlino*, the local rag.

Background on Signor Fuoco. When did Lucia splash on the Bologna scene?

Early afternoon, I visited Il Pastificio Gustare. Its reputation was deserved, a temple to Ceres. The mosaic floor depicted the goddess of food. Glass cases lined with pasta purses filled with zucchini blossoms, triangles with four kinds of mushrooms, linguine in five colors, tagliatelle and tortellini. I asked for the manager. A round man scurried out from the back, small eyes peering out of a floury face.

"We haven't seen Giancarlo and we're worried. We're having trouble with the tortellini he created two weeks ago. This new shape, we can't get the twist right."

"Tell me, do you remember a woman who bought here frequently, tall, dark hair, well dressed, talked to Giancarlo?"

He looked puzzled. "Which one?"

"What do you mean? This one would be very hard to miss."

"He always has expensive good looking dames around."

Giancarlo was lousy when it came to business. His rich lady friends kept the place afloat. When he ran out of money he'd find a new dame to invest.

* * *

My pal in Venice said Lucia, nee Monti, had been at the convent, but left when she was fourteen, not eighteen, with an English family. Her grandmother gave permission. The nuns said she went to London with her friend. The society gal at *Il Resto* said Lucia arrived in town about seven years ago. No one was able to uncover much about her background, only some talk about being seen in the company of different men from time to time on via della Spiga, the fashion walk in Milan. Her beauty and warm manner with other women captured the hearts of il bel mondo. Marriage to a bank president capped an obvious quest.

* * *

Next morning, feet up on the desk, reading the papers. *Il Resto del Carlino*, shouted "Gustare Body Found." A gardener stumbled over the corpse in the park surrounding the church of Madonna di San Luca on the hill. Gustare had been strangled and then stabbed according to the carabinieri. The national papers, *La Repubblica* and *La Stampa*, speculated on what might have happened to a Sicilian pasta maker who found fame in the tightly knit coterie of specialists in Bologna.

The door clattered and I jumped up. Signora Fuoco rushed in and threw her arms around my neck.

"Gianni, find the killer. I'm afraid. The papers this morning. I scarcely made it through breakfast."

My arms only reluctantly released the fire they held. For safety, I moved to my side of the desk. She sat and crossed her legs. The thrilling sibilance of silk against silk.

"Luigi reads the paper during breakfast. This morning he put it down and looked at me strangely. 'This man that's missing, that's where you've been buying the pasta, no?'

"He went back to reading the paper and didn't say anything more. As he was leaving, 'I had the cook buy some tortellini while you were away. It did not please me.'"

"Signora, have the police been to see you? You were the last person with Giancarlo. You could be a suspect."

"No one knew I was there, no one. Not even his killers."

"Your husband? I think somehow he found out what was going on and decided to eliminate Giancarlo."

"Luigi has been jealous. He frowns when I talk too long to other men at the opera. But he has never been violent. He's a banker."

"Yesterday, I asked you if he could have noticed anything, when you were alone."

A pink tint rose in her cheeks. "Every Sunday before we go to church he comes to my room. I lie there. First, he gazes at my stomach, (she dropped her eyes), caresses it, touches my navel, (her hand moved down), then comes into me. And it's over."

She shook her head two or three times to erase the thought.

"Not to be indelicate, but that's all? How old did you say your husband was?"

"I do not wish to speak ill of Luigi, but life is not very fulfilling for a young woman married to an older man whose greatest interests in life are banking and soccer."

"There's no way he, or your servant, or anyone, could have followed you and Giancarlo?"

"We were careful. We went separately and met at different times."

She looked at me expectantly. Some long seconds passed. "Gianni, I could use a drink."

I got up and came around the desk. She rose in my path. We stood, not an inch apart. "Please, I can't live like this. Take care of me."

Yes, I would, of course I would, for as long as wine was red.

Crossing the street, we kept a deliberate distance from each other. The caffè on via Farini was a dark little place with stained wooden tables and chairs. We settled in a quiet corner. Lingered. I reached across and touched her hand. We said little, looked into one another's eyes, electricity sparking, ions colliding. A crush of patrons broke our reverie. She got up, breathed a kiss that brushed my lips, and left.

* * *

I was baffled. The controlling banker was the most likely suspect, tough enough, and he certainly had the contacts and money. I couldn't imagine he did the job himself. So how would a banker meet a hit man? I went over to see his driver, Massimo, again. This time with a friendly 100 euro note in my handshake.

"Lunch time, I pick up the clients, bring them here, then take them back."

"Anyone remarkable?"

"Blue suits, white shirts, silver ties usually. But last week, two new ones: younger, big guys, silk shirts and no ties. One had a gimpy left leg, the other had a raw scar on his cheek. Movie people I think. Talked like they were in mafia films."

I checked out the building where Massimo picked up and dropped the movie men: two ad agencies, an insurance company, and lawyers' offices. I hung around for two days. No signs of them.

* * *

I walked over to Al Cappello Rosso about the time the maids would be leaving for the day. At four o'clock three women left the hotel by a side door, slumping, trodding along in comfortable shoes, hair somewhat disheveled. The older of the three lagged behind.

"Madame, may I have a word with you? I have heard that the man found dead at Madonna di San Luca came to the hotel sometimes."

"I know nothing. The customers are not my business, especially when I'm not getting paid."

"Not paid?"

"Not for three weeks. My husband is crippled. I hardly have enough for soup."

"The hotel looks like it does well."

"The owner has financial problems. He borrowed money from the bank, that one over on Piazza Maggiore they say, and cannot pay."

"A pity, a man with a fine hotel, making his workers suffer. Will you accept twenty euros so you can have some meat for your husband tonight?"

"God bless you, sir."

* * *

I couldn't prove Signor Fuoco had his wife's lover murdered and covered up. At the same time, I couldn't shake the feeling Lucia may have played on the heart strings of a jealous husband and needy lover. Sitting in my office, going over notes, she walked in. A vision to make angels weep. Her hair piled on top of her head. A black suit designed on her body.

"There is a quiet place where we can talk more openly. Meet me at the Majestic in twenty minutes. Suite Verdi, third floor. The door will be open."

She turned and left.

I walked as calmly as I could the three hundred meters from my office, past the two leaning towers, to the hotel. Suite Verdi took up half the floor. A large door opened to a sitting room of cream colored walls with gilt and green accents and 17th century Dutch paintings. Lucia stood in the middle of the room, no shoes, feet slightly apart.

"Come in, Gianni."

I nodded and grinned, probably too much. She pulled a comb from her hair, tossed her head, and long black hair tumbled over her left shoulder. With what appeared to be a shudder, her jacket dropped to the floor, nothing beneath it but a bountiful bare breasted woman. She smiled, then shook her hips and the skirt slipped to the floor. I could do no more than gape. She pursed her lips, whispered "follow me," turned and opened the door to a bedroom adorned in gold and mirrors.

She lay on her side in bed as I fumbled getting out of my suit. Shoe laces never loosen easily at these times. Finally, I moved in beside her and kissed my way down every inch of her velvety body. At her navel I stopped, gasped, hopefully so slightly she didn't notice. There, a navel formed by Venus, I had seen before.

In the pastificio. Giancarlo had fashioned a tortellini in the shape of Lucia's navel, a tribute to its singular beauty. While she visited her nonna in Venice, Signor Fuoco's cook bought the tortellini. Signor Fuoco recognized his wife's navel and knew only one way the pasta maker knew that shape, a long thin opening with a perceptible left twist.

Afterward, lying in bed I placed the tortellini on her stomach. Side by side, I admired the pasta maker's skill.

"What is that?"

"It's what killed Giancarlo."

"What?"

She didn't know Giancarlo shaped a tortellini for her?

Then I explained how her husband found out and described the movie types Massimo had picked up.

"There were two men at the end of the lane when I went into the hotel last week. Dear God, those were the ones."

* * *

Things moved fast. I described the men to my friend Nico in the carabinieri. The two guys had been under surveillance for some time for three or four different jobs. The hit men ratted the banker out at the trial. Lucia's reputation, and/or the banker's virility, might have been compromised, but the judge and lawyers were persuaded to limit prosecution testimony to the hit men. Their attestations detailed only their meeting with Signor Fuoco, the exchange of euros, and manner of the strangling and stabbing. Later, I found out from Nico that Gustare died from strangulation. The stabbing was ordered by the banker to scare his wife. The motive for the killing and the name of the hotel were deemed irrelevant and the banker did not testify. He took up residence at La Dozza Prison.

* * *

I hadn't seen Lucia since the trial. Her lawyer advised we stay apart. I was hanging around the office when she called and invited me to dinner. Her apartment took up the top floor of a building overlooking the river valleys at the southern end of the city. The door opened to a décor of drop cloths, ladders, and boxes of hi-tech security equipment.

"Excuse the mess. I decided to clear out the 18th century and bring the apartment into the 21st."

She took my hand and led me into the study, still in the earlier century with dark cedar walls and gloomy tapestries. After champagne, dinner was brought in and set on a small table. When she dismissed the maid, my hopes rose.

"Here's your last payment. A little extra, you did well."

A fat envelope. Visions of how the evening might unfold began to play in my head. As we ate, she talked about Luigi. Not doing well. The stress of the ordeal had unhinged him, mentally and physically.

She paused and I rose from my chair and lifted her into my arms.

"Oh Gianni, not tonight, I have an early train to Milan. Meetings with lawyers and accountants about the estate. It is so much larger than I imagined."

She took a step back, her eyes, once warm pools of promise, now looked like the Arctic Sea. I too had been part of her performance, but now the curtain falls.

Mia

New York, Recently

He was a sweet lay. Charlie, that's what he said his name was, picked me up at The Pub. He thought he did the picking, but then most guys do. The Pub, a neighborhood bar on the upper West Side, heavy on the wood, pretenses of being English, dart board, shepherd pie, cheese and chutney nibbles. I was perched on a stool at the bar with a Vodka Collins. He was at the far end, a lean 6'2", sandy hair, horn rims. I turned his way once or twice, rested my eyes, not waiting to see if he noticed. He finished his beer, walked toward the door, stopped.

"Looks like heaven's missing an angel," he said.

"Think you've got that one turned around."

"I can go either way."

"If I can't?"

"Then it's the devil's way."

Light played off his smile and I thought, what the hell. He took my hand and we strolled back to his place, a block away. Nice, but a heavy decorator's hand: black and white Montmartre street photos, leather, plaid throws.

I liked Charlie, Charlie with the green eyes that told stories of mischief, the kid who peeked while his teen-age sister's friend was taking a shower. He lit the logs in the fireplace, we sipped cognac, and he un-wrapped me, quickly, and a little rough. Sometimes, this time, a turn-on. Then he took his time as his lips moved slowly from my breasts to my belly to below. At each stop, he inscribed little circles of pleasure with his tongue.

In the second act, we traded places and I felt the heat from his smooth skin and savored his cedar smell as I licked my way down his body. After the third act, he fell asleep. I waited an hour, got up, dressed, and left. It had been a perfectly cozy tumble on a rainy night, but I had places to go and people to kill.

K, the guy that saved my ass at Maroun al-Ras, now with Mossad, had called late that afternoon. Asked if I'd do him a favor. A major problem with a Russian named Sergei R. in Brighton Beach.

"Can't you get the FBI to arrest him?"

"Tried that," K said. "For the last two years, but they're not buying the evidence we've collected, claim it's weak."

"And it's not?"

"It's solid, Mia, I promise."

Not something I'd ordinarily do. After my tour, I thought I never wanted to kill anyone again. What good did it do? But I owed K, and there a good reason this Sergei R. should die. He was the state-side link of a sex slave trade triangle run out of Kiev into Tel Aviv on to

New York. Roma girls were recruited on the pretext of becoming nannies, then sold off to pimps in the Midwest. K would take care of the Ukrainian and Israeli angles if I'd handle this one. No one else was going to stop this, only K and me.

We need to back up here. Out of Wharton I wanted a job on the Street, had a couple of offers—Morgan, Merrill, but then the market went in the tank, and when the tank broke, it was: we'd-love-to-have-you-and-we're-sure-business-will-pick-up-in-six-months-but-at-the-moment . . . So I did what every Jewish girl with an MBA/JD does, went to Israel to do the kibbutz thing. Don't they? Some do, if their grandparents were kibbutzniks.

Six months in the kibbutz when an army recruiter came through with stories about the exploits of the Israeli Defense Force. I knew the story. My grandparents had talked about being rescued back in '49. I signed up for a two-year stint. An added attraction, the training base was near Haifa—cypress trees, rain, lush green hills, beaches, and men.

In basic, it turned out I was a crack shot. Top of the class. Qualified for sniper school. There, I graduated second. A natural talent it seemed. Two things: metabolism of a cat and people with gray eyes have better vision, more light gets through. And to do something with impact. In the lingo, be a force multiplier. Eliminate commanding officers and the people manning the serious weapons.

My first action, Lebanon. Beautiful country – the crenelated landscape painted with deep green valleys and framed by pale gray limestone cliffs, but marred by villages with broken buildings and rubble from shelling. My Recon Company was sent in to Maroun al-Ras with K as my partner. We set up on a high point, a place with good sight lines. K was about 20 feet to my right. The field we overlooked was target rich. Out 500 meters were four Fajr-5 rocket launchers and their crews. I'd taken out the three crew members on the nearest launcher. I could see the faces of the soldiers I killed, but didn't allow myself to get distracted. I targeted a button on their chest and believed if I didn't kill them, women and children would die. And I tell myself that every time a settlement takes a round.

I set up for the next launcher crew, heard the brush crackle on my left, turned, a dark hulk, blotting out the sun, a man, head wrapped in a black scarf, a long knife, a whisper,

"Hot-me-et-un-mote! Die!"

My stomach clutched. I'd been triangulated *So fucking stupid, Mia. Lesson one, shoot, move.* I was dug in, arms trapped by my rifle. I couldn't budge. I screamed, but nothing came out. Then, a shot, a knife clanked off my helmet, a man fell on my legs.

"Stay down, Mia," K yelled. Then ran up and finished off the attacker with his bayonet.

My two years in the IDF up, I came back to the city. The economy still sucked and the Street wasn't hiring. I had a bit saved, so I hung with some people from B-school, made a serious study of the after-hours clubs and the guys who go there. Some rough characters. Wolves in Street clothing. I hit the gym for a couple of hours in the afternoon and had my weekly mani-pedi.

I interrupted the Sergei R. story for some background. Now back to him. It took a few days to find him in Asser Levy Park. A stocky man, mid 50s, pasty complexion, sour expression, a track suit, finger thick gold chain and black leather shoes—Russian mafia couture. I sat on a bench watching. The first morning, as a mother cooing to her baby swaddled in a blanket. Another morning, as a thread-bare homeless woman with an overflowing shopping cart. Sergei had a pattern. At seven every morning he walked his overweight toy poodle. Seemed to love the little thing. Picked him up, nuzzled him, fed him tiny biscuits.

The Park was bounded by high rises on one side, (he lived in 8905), and four-lane Surf Boulevard, behind Coney Island beach. A park saturated by ocean humidity and salt. Sergei walked the same paths, always, the ones between the amphitheater and the road. Not many people and not many cars early in the day, especially when the fog hung low.

I spent time mapping sight lines and covers. Found a grove of trees with the perfect angle. Waited for a rainy day. Bullets shoot flatter (more accurately), and footprints would be washed out. I went to Goodwill and picked up two long raincoats, standard tan and a pair of boots.

The rain started at four Wednesday morning. I was ready. When I saw him at the end of the path, I pulled the rifle from under my coats, lay down in the mud, set the bipod, adjusted the scope, a little to the left, for spin drift. Nailed him at 200 meters. He flopped, fortunately not on top of the little dog. A couple of days later, an envelope under the door. From K. Generous, down payment on a West Side two bedroom. That knife that clanked off my helmet, I hung it over my bed.

A month after the Russian job, K called again. "I hate to ask this, but Mia, one more. Please."

"What's it about this time?"

"Guy molesting my cousin. She works for him in the Diamond District, forcing her to do things to him. Disgusting things. Even you, I can't say the words to."

"Why doesn't she . . ."

"Forget the cops, my cousin told me the guy is a big contributor to Orphans and Widows. Is that something?"

"Listen K, some things I can't kill for. Only one person involved here. Sorry, I know it's your cousin, but for me it's got to be proportional. What I will do is put him in pain for a long while."

My plan, take out his knee. I checked and he didn't have insurance. Friend over at Aetna ran a cross company search. Thing they did when anybody applied. Made sure people weren't double and triple insuring for the same thing. This jewelry guy would be forced to sell the business to cover multiple operations. K's cousin would be home free.

Isaac lived over in Borough Park and spent time strolling in nearby Green-Wood Cemetery after he closed-up shop on 47th Street. On a path below a rise covered with poplars, dotted with small crypts. One evening at dusk, from behind a red granite tombstone, Sloat (Rear Admiral, claimed California for the U.S., according to Wikipedia) was the name on the plinth, at 100 meters, I took out his right knee. The shot was true, but when I turned around, I saw a pale faced man in a green uniform and service cap, cemetery custodian on rounds, about fifty feet away, staring at me. He twisted around to pull a walkie-talkie from the holster on his belt. *Where the shit did he come from? Think Mia. Make him forget.* I set my rifle down, unbuttoned my coat and my blouse and let my skirt slip down my legs. Then picked up the rifle, walked toward him, unhooked my lacy red bra, opened it, started to slide my panties, red also, over my hips. He gasped, turned, dropped the walkie-talkie, stumbled, pulled himself up, and ran. He won't remember my face.

Justice frontier style, but justice all the same for the Roma girls and K's cousin. Talked to a rabbi about the Torah's "eye for an eye." It came down to guys who batter their wives, abuse kids, and stalk women. The city needed its modern day paladin, not the *Dungeons and Dragons* video game variety. Not trying to subvert the legal system, just give victims a righteous response. Why me? I'm smart and educated, dispassionate (some of my school friends have said 'cold') and I can shoot. I didn't want to do it. I had to do it. All that, plus memories of the time I spent on the kibbutz at Yahel. Up before dawn to milk, lead the cows out to pasture, muck out the stalls, bring the cows back in. And repeat. It's kind of corny, but my milk fed babies. I'd felt part of something larger than my own family. It seemed more important than a career in finance.

* * *

Charlie was gone a month, business trip to the coast. Back in town, apologized for the silence, invited me to *Behanding in Seattle*. He did a great Christopher Walken low raspy, "I don't need to be made (pause) to look evil. I can do that (pause) on my own." Also spent time with his brother who lived in San Francisco. Went on about how his brother had become bearable, even likeable since he'd married and had a kid. Charlie liked kids. Twice a week he coached for the Police Athletic League up on 119th Street. He'd been all-conference guard at Bucknell. Good hands (to which I could attest). They seemed large for a man just over six feet.

Meantime, I decided to become a PI. License to carry. I'd investigate first, fire only if I had to. The PI exam was a doodle and I managed to convince the examiner that my military service met the experience requirements. A friend from Wharton worked for Della Femina, the ad agency, and helped me put together a media campaign focused on women's issues—cheating husbands, abusive partners. The image: hip, hard, helping.

Over on 47th and Second, west side of the street, gold lettering on a third-story window.

ALLAN & MONROE

PRIVATE INVESTIGATORS

FOR HIRE

That's my office. I'm the Allan, Miriam Ivanna. It's been Mia since I left home. There's no Monroe, never was, but a double-barrel name is reassuring. That's what the Marketing prof at Wharton said, though I don't think he had this in mind.

A couple of weeks later, raining, Charlie and I grabbed a cab to see *View from the Bridge.* Cabbie missed the turn on 45th. Charlie went crazy. Nearly jumped into the front seat. Thought he would throttle the driver, but I managed to grab his arm. When he sat back, he became all apologetic, to me and when we got out, he gave the cabbie a fifty. A little class to Charlie, more than just good in the sack. Okay, hair-trigger temper, but cooled quickly. Occupational hazard probably. A stockbroker, started with Salomon, now Morgan Stanley. Successful, smooth talker. I wasn't in a hurry to settle down with anyone, but he made me start to think about it. Never fails when you spend your summer weekends at girl-friends' weddings.

* * *

Late one afternoon, a woman poked her head in my office door. Late-twenties, black hair, spikey, contrasted with a blue polka dot shirt dress. Nina Silvano seemed both nervous and determined. Sat very straight in the chair.

"The night before last, I was in this bar, The Pub, and I'm afraid I had a bit too much to drink after Roger didn't show."

"Happens to all of us. The Pub, the one over on the West Side?"

"Yeah, that one. Anyway, this cute guy, I'd seen him there before, convinced me to go home with him. When I got outside, the rain woke me up and I decided I didn't want to."

"So?"

"When I told him, he went nutso and shoved me against the building, then grabbed my arms, held my wrists above my head with one hand."

"Which hand?"

"I'm pretty sure it was his left hand." She showed me the bruises, turning yellow and green. I looked carefully.

The marks were from a left-hand clutch. His thumb left a distinctive mark. "He put his other hand over my mouth."

She stomped on the guy's shoe, he let go for a minute, and she ran into the street just as a cab passed. I asked her what she wanted me to do.

"Remember, last week in the paper, the girl that was found strangled on the west side of Central Park? I'm afraid it might be the same guy."

"Why?"

"I'd been to The Pub the night of the murder, saw the girl there, I saw him too. According to the papers she had bruises on her wrists when she was found, like mine."

"That's not much to go on."

"But, when they were sitting in the corner, they argued, waved their hands. After five minutes of this they quieted down, then he kissed her palm and she leaned into him. After that she went to the bar and talked to, I guess, a girlfriend. On his way out, he stopped and said something to her. She nodded, like she was agreeing to meet him because a couple of minutes later, she left too."

"Okay, let's start with the basics—Name? What did he look like? Age? What was he wearing? Anything quirky about him?"

"Danny was over six feet, kind of built, sandy hair, horn rims. Maybe in his mid-thirties. And he wore a soft leather jacket."

"Did you notice the color of his eyes?"

"They were green, beautiful actually."

She waited for me to say something.

"What's the matter?" she asked.

"Nothing, nothing at all."

"One other thing. He left before me. He said he was going to step out of the bar and call his brother. Something to do with him coming to town. Danny wanted me to meet him at the corner. That's where he grabbed me."

"Did you talk to the police? The Central Park murder story has been all over the papers."

"They said they had it under control. The cop heading up the investigation said they'd identified *persons of interest*. I spent an hour with them but it seemed they only wanted to hear things that confirmed what they already knew."

I helped Nina to the door, a sisterly hug, and said I'd see what I could do.

I checked out Nina and Charlie, their college and job records, co-workers, past lovers, friends. Spent a month, following them around and digging through computer files. My client was as close as you can come to a convent girl, these days. Sacred Heart for high school, Marymount, and now fifth grade teacher at Blessed Sacrament over on West 70th. And I dug into the background of the woman who'd been murdered—mid-twenties, black hair, pale complexion, graduated NYU in sociology, worked for the city. Seemed Charlie had a thing for black hair, pale complexioned women.

Turned out Charlie's name was Daniel Xavier O'Rourke. For someone his age, had the usual number of affairs, only one went as far as an engagement. Nothing to suggest he'd beat a woman. And I couldn't hold a phony name against someone. Well, maybe I could, three months?

I went into the Pub before the crowd one night and talked to the bartender. He remembered that the victim and Charlie/Danny had both been in the bar the night of the murder, but he saw them together for only a minute. Busy night. The bartender did remember Charlie paid his tab and left. Sometime later, the woman hurried out. After a month of sleuthing, I understood the police position. Too much coincidence for them, for me too.

I had to be sure, for me, and for my client. Knew I could bump into Charlie at The Pub without making it obvious what I was up to. I wore my pencil leg pants, heels, and a black silk blouse with a serious V. He was by himself at a table in the corner. Cords, brown bomber jacket, sipping a Guinness. He called out as I walked in.

"Where have you been?" He stood and took both my hands in his. "I've missed you."

"Business trips. Quieted down a bit now."

"You never told me what you do." He seemed genuinely interested.

"We had other things to talk about."

"So, what is it you do?"

"You want to continue the conversation at my place?" I said. After all, he was only a suspect, no proof of guilt, yet.

He threw a fifty on the table and we left. He placed

my arm on his and kissed my hair as we walked back to my apartment. Sweet gesture.

Pleasure first. Act One played out as always. Very, very nice. Then business. I went a little mean on him. "Is that all you got?" Poked him in the ribs. He looked startled. "Where'd you leave the big man?" Light cuff on the ear. He turned red.

"What the hell's this?"

He jumped out of bed, pulling the blanket with him. His back to me. He must be into a new weight routine—the traps had more definition, and his ass was definitely tighter than I remembered. I watched, lying on the bed propped up on my right elbow, sheets pulled up. I could tell he was tense the way his muscles bunched, but he didn't say anything, not even heavy breathing. He stuffed his shorts into the pocket of his pants, put his left leg through them, teetered a bit as his lost his balance, then stuck his right leg through. Maybe Charlie could control himself. He wasn't the killer.

"You always leave your women disappointed?"

He continued to dress, reached down for his shirt, put his right arm in the sleeve, hesitated, let the shirt drop, then whirled around, his face livid. Before I could move, his fist smashed into my cheek.

"Bitch!"

I scurried and rolled across the bed, but got caught in the sheets. With his left hand, he grabbed my right wrist, then the left one, and squeezed them together. Punched me in the stomach. His hands were around my throat, pushing down. I groped for the drawer in the bedside table and knocked the lamp on the floor. He jerked. Cold steel pushed into his gut. My .38.

"Whoa, baby," I purred. I wanted him to remember I don't scare.

He stumbled for the door. I think his shirt was on backward and he left his socks on the carpet. Yup. Charlie had a mean streak, deep and ugly. And the mirror said my face wore it. Shit! It hurt. *Why Charlie? Why is it you? Why didn't I see it?*

Much later, I figured out it was me. Out to have fun, grab it when I could, hell with consequences. That's what happened with Charlie.

But, his taste in women, his M.O. He was the one, but not enough hard facts to go to the police. But this violence. Couldn't watch him all the time. Couldn't risk other women. I had to. Next Wednesday, I'll be in position on Summit Rock in Central Park. First light. Charlie will jog from his apartment on West 80th, toward the Reservoir. He'll run towards the Rock. Me, I'll be kneeling in the shadows, arm vertical under my rifle, I'll see him, I'll sight on his heart, I'll count down, I'll feel the heat of the target, I'll remember the smell of the target, I'll breathe in, let out half a breath, I'll be in my still place, steady pressure to the very end of my finger.

The bullet will travel through his heart faster than the speed at which his tissues tear, stretching them beyond their breaking points. His blood pressure will drop quickly, but it will take 10 to 15 seconds for him to lose brain function. Time to think about why this is happening to him.

Christopher
Faversham, Kent, England, Recently

She was sprawled across the path. Pale skin, ebony curls, and a crimson gown against the green mossy stone. I turned and saw the husband seated nearby. A dark-haired fellow, clothed in a silk dressing gown and black velvet slippers, head tilted back to enjoy the patter of rain, the scent of mown grass, and the blush of rose petals in early morning, only occasionally glancing at his wife's body.

"Sir." I tried to focus the man's attention. "I am Detective Chief Inspector Christopher Turney, Kent Police."

"Ironic," Richard Carlyle said, "Francesca dead, unable to share this splendid morning."

I tried again to shake Carlyle from his reverie, "Sir, when did you discover your wife's body?"

"Oh yes, well, I arrived home last evening before she did, woke to find her missing from her bed, searched the house, combed the grounds, then came out here. She rather favored this small garden, you know."

Carlyle spoke little, perhaps mindful that when one speaks, one often says too much.

"Why hadn't you come home together?"

"Happened often. Different tolerance for jollity, that sort of thing."

There were no marks on Francesca Carlyle's face, hands, or shoulders. The gown was not ripped or stained. Her face betrayed only an expression of slight surprise. The medical examiner peered closely, said, "Nothing to indicate violence or death by other than natural causes. We'll have more, early afternoon."

Carlyle pointed to a slate blue falcon resting on a post under the eaves of a shed at the end of the garden. "Francesca named her Mabel. I find few women are content without an interest, it matters little what—flowers, be they roses or hydrangeas; animals, horses or dogs; or friends, card playing or shopping—as long as pursued avidly. My wife found hers in falcons."

"Excuse me sir, but your wife is dead, most unexpectedly. She's lying here in front of you, and you are talking about birds."

"Yes, the bird business started after she had been up to London one day. At the Wallace, she saw Vernet's *An Algerian Lady Hawking*." He turned toward me. "Have you seen it? Um, perhaps not." I feigned indifference at the slight. "It portrays a woman, a princess I believe, in a flowing gossamer blouse, astride a magnificent white steed, seated on a crimson saddle, with a bird on the hand. This became Francesca's new self-image."

Little point continuing the conversation. Reality had

slipped from Carlyle's grasp. I told my men to trawl the house and grounds for clues. Carlyle requested only that they complete their work in the small garden first. He intended to do some pruning and talk to Mabel about the morning. "Figuratively, you understand, Chief Inspector."

"I'll be leaving one of my men here, Mr. Carlyle, to see evidence is not disturbed."

* * *

I returned to Pembroke Hall a little past two. In the house, white flowers replaced the multi-hued ones there this morning. Carlyle, now dressed in riding clothes, sat at a small table in the garden, nibbling on cheese and slices of cold beef. A bottle of claret caught the light, perhaps a glass left.

"Sorry to disturb your lunch, but I thought you would be interested in the medical examiner's preliminary findings."

Carlyle tilted his chair back and put his feet on the table. "I was reminiscing about the times we vacationed in Morocco and India. That lovely hotel with the tiled arcade in Marrakesh, the chalk white inn above the caravan route at Ouarzazate, the palace in Jaipur with peacocks performing at breakfast, and a subterranean blue and gold mosaic lined pool. One misses those things. Since the bird arrived a year ago, those adventures have been curtailed. Haven't been anywhere. Not that Mabel couldn't have been sheltered with a fellow falconer."

"Your wife died of asphyxiation. Most likely, someone smothered her. The examiner found some bluish discoloration around her mouth and nose, something we didn't observe in morning light. Also, congestion in the nose and sinus — typical in these cases."

"So she stopped breathing."

"Was stopped from breathing, sir."

Carlyle nodded.

"And it seems she had consumed a considerable quantity of alcohol."

"Not unusual."

"May I ask about the relationship between you and your late wife?"

"We lived together."

"Is that all?"

"What more can one say?"

I stared out the window. A deer bounded across the lawn. This chap seemed two biscuits short of a tin. "Tell me, Mr. Carlyle who would want your wife dead?"

"I haven't the faintest idea. None whatsoever." Carlyle paused. "I don't suppose that affair in London could have come back to haunt her. You remember, some ten years ago, Sir George Bagot, Defense Secretary Thomson, and the two young Italian girls. She was Francesca Scarletti then."

I did recall the scandal about government funds finding their way into a sham company insuring completion of a military project in Egypt. "We'll look into it, but after this time, I'm sure most of the actors have moved on."

I made to leave, put my hand in my pocket for the keys and came on the envelope. "Oh, my people found this in the bookcase. From the Royal Society for the Protection of Birds addressed to Mrs. Carlyle. Do you know anything about it? Appears not to have been opened."

Carlyle turned, leaned forward, glanced at the envelope, then shrugged. "Only that Francesca was quite keen. I've never seen it before."

* * *

With Carlyle's preoccupation with the falcon, I rang up Mr. Elliott, a falconer of local repute. According to him, Francesca Carlyle had devoted hours to Mabel: manning her, which he told me meant the bird became acculturated to humans, accustomed to the falconer and learned to associate food with the glove. Then trained her to hunt: the jesses and creances. Finally, she bought a telemetry transmitter for free flight hunting.

"She was uncommonly proud of that bird. When Mabel killed her first pigeon, Mrs. Carlyle had a taxidermist mount one of the prey's wings. All that was left." The disapproving curl of the lip audible over the phone.

Elliott had been present at a recent meeting of the local chapter of the Royal Society for the Protection of Birds when Mrs. Carlyle walked in. The plight of the northern harrier was discussed. The impending loss of its habitat in Scotland to building speculators aroused the birding contingent.

"The lady pledged some millions of pounds against the purchase of land for a sanctuary. As if the sum were a pittance." Days after the meeting, Elliott was still unable to recount the event without stumbling over his words.

Mrs. Carlyle was promptly promised ("though not guaranteed," Elliott noted) a presentation to the Queen and perhaps an C.B.E. for her generosity, as Her Majesty is patron of the RSPB. It was common knowledge in falconry circles that Francesca was keen on being Dame Francesca. After hanging up, I put Sergeant Albert Sellman, one of my brighter lads, up from Cambridge, on the trail of the Carlyle finances.

* * *

Next morning, I came back to the Hall and found Carlyle in the library studying a racing form. I had more questions. Could Carlyle prove he came directly home? Never left his bed until morning?

No, he could not corroborate his movements. He recited events as they occurred: he and his wife went to the ball. Sipped champagne. Danced. Dined on pheasant. Played cards (he, whist, she, bridge). Heavy stakes at the bridge table required she stay longer and so he left and went home to bed.

"The Moncrieffs, I believe it was Sara, or perhaps Hugh, I'm not sure who volunteered to bring her home."

"Did you sleep soundly?" I asked, wondering how natural the reply might be.

"I did. I'd been riding earlier in the day with some younger fellows and they rather extended me." Carlyle sat back in his chair, thinking I'd be satisfied with the reply.

"Their names, please."

"What? You doubt me?" Carlyle sat up, as if restored to horseback.

"In cases like this, we need to verify everything. Speaking of which, as your wife seems to have been suffocated, we'll be sending the cushions and pillows in the sitting room and library to the laboratory in London to examine them for fingerprints and fluids."

"Why London?"

"Special equipment. Quite new. The materials are placed in a vacuum chamber, gold is heated up and spread like a film over the fabric. Then zinc is heated. It attaches to the gold where there are no fingerprint residues. The fingerprints are revealed against the fabric. Somewhat like a photo negative."

"I see," Carlyle said, and turned back to the racing form.

* * *

Sellman stumbled into my office, a jumble of chairs and filing cabinets, all dominated by my large wooden desk piled high with files. The walls were covered with some of my water colors of the Lake District. A few ribbons at local shows, I might add.

I persuaded Mrs. Carlyle's solicitor to share with me the principal terms of her will.

"Good show, Albert."

"A small annuity to Mabel. Pieces of jewelry to her mother. The flat on Eaton Place, number 31 (three units in addition to one below stairs) and five million pounds in Treasury bonds were left to her husband. And, the contents of a safe deposit box and numbered account in a Swiss bank to a woman in Bologna."

"Someone connected to the Thomson affair, I presume. You know it?"

"Actually, I do," Sellman said. "Case study in international public finance at university."

Sellman rushed on. "And I know you're not interested and it's probably not relevant, but I found out that number 31 has a bit of a history. Alan Lerner wrote the lyrics for *My Fair Lady* in the upper maisonette and Jeremy Thorpe, the Liberal leader, kept the below stairs flat for his assignations with other men."

"No, not relevant, but an interesting sidelight, if one is fond of the West End, or politics."

"Yes sir."

"The amount on the RSPB pledge form would have left Carlyle a poor man. I wonder if he could have held on to Pembroke Hall?"

"I suppose he was aware of the pledge."

"Elliott, the falconer, was there when she pledged the money. He has the distinct impression that it was a spur of the moment thing."

"So it would appear that since, or because of, the death of his wife, Mr. Carlyle is without a financial care."

"It would."

* * *

As I walked up the path to the Moncrieff's manor, the scene of Mrs. Carlyle's last party, shouts and cries came from inside. I rapped on the door, wasn't heard over the barking man and bawling woman, I rapped again, finally pushed the door, found it unlocked, and hesitantly stepped into the foyer. Sara and Hugh Moncrieff stood at opposite ends of the space framed by tall arches, open mouthed, red faced, whirling their arms, hurling invectives at one another. As they caught sight of me, they quieted.

"Am I interrupting?"

"Please, do come in." Mrs. Moncrieff swept her welcoming arms towards a nearby room. Curiously furnished with low slung white leather and chrome sofas and chairs. The high ceilings and Regency molding miniaturized the furniture and the people.

"You're here about our dear Francesca, I'm sure."

Sara Moncrieff was a tall willowy woman, chestnut hair, and freckled, more and more apparently as the angry red drained down to her neck and chest. I noticed her arms, the prominent musculature of a horsewoman. We went into the library where we sat around a low mahogany table.

"Something to drink, Chief Inspector?" Moncrieff offered heartily, as if to a long lost friend.

"Water will be fine."

"A sherry," she said.

Moncrieff returned, balancing a tray with my water, his wife's sherry, and a tumbler of whiskey. He offered sharp contrast to his wife: short, stocky, bright blue eyes, and broken-blood-vessel ruddy cheeks.

"Before we talk of the night of Francesca Carlyle's murder, what do you know about them?"

Sara Moncrieff started. "Richard found her somewhere on the Cote d'Azur, lying low after the scandal in London. You know the one?"

I nodded.

"They were the perfect match—she was pretty, vivacious and had a bundle, apparently a payoff. He was landed gentry in a quiet spot of the country, sophisticated, with a manor going…" she paused.

Her husband barged in, "Say it, dammit woman, Pembroke Hall was going to ruins. The disgrace of the county."

This confirmed what Carlyle told me and what I'd picked up from an internet search and chats with villagers about Pembroke.

"Another thing, do either of you know why Mrs. Carlyle might have been particularly keen on a C.B.E.?"

"Wanted to lord it over that Bagot chap," Sarah said. "We were in London one afternoon shopping, passed his office in Knightsbridge. She squeaked, 'How rich if he had to address me as Dame Francesca.'"

"Coming back to the night of your ball, Mr. Carlyle said one of you offered to drive his wife back to Pembroke. He had left earlier."

"You have it turned around, Chief Inspector," Moncrieff said, "She left first. Richard wanted to stay on."

"I see. But, which of you drove her?"

"Was it you, Hugh darling?" with an emphasis on 'darling' that suggested the contrary.

"Don't you remember, it was you, old girl," he snapped.

"Why it was. I had to help poor Francesca up the outside stairs and ended up setting her down in a chair in the library. I simply couldn't carry her further."

"Did you see anyone? She was found in the garden."

"I know, poor thing. No one, but then I'd drunk a bit more than usual."

"Then what, darling?" Moncrieff interjected.

"Usual. So you see Chief Inspector, a thing or two may have escaped me."

"Or many things," Moncrieff added.

"Darling," she insisted, "we have a guest."

I stood up and walked about, to create a different mood. "So it appears you were the last to see her alive."

"Oh dear, I hope I said something nice to her." Sara Moncrieff twisted her hands as if perhaps she hadn't.

"I'm sure you did," her husband said. "You are always considerate and sweet tempered to the wives of your male friends."

"Especially in these times," she said.

"These times?"

I lost the thread of the conversation, but it was worth letting them continue with their rant. Moncrieff leaned forward, face flushed from having consumed the tumbler of whiskey. "Our Francesca had become quite batty these recent months. The falcon, then this affectation of a North African princess, the kind Delacroix was fond of."

"Why yes, I've seen them at his small museum in Paris."

"You have," in a tone that anticipated I hadn't been to Paris.

"Well, quite a sight, our Francesca, not an unpleasing one though, I'd say. Most grating for Richard was her refusal to ever leave the bird."

"Poor Richard, his life turned upside down," Mrs. Moncrieff added.

"Ah yes, poor Richard, who must be at every function we hold, so extraordinarily handsome, such a conversationalist, life of the party, according to my Sara, who knows him intimately."

She got up from her chair and walked to the end of the room. "What is that supposed to mean?"

"I'm not sure it is relevant to the Chief Inspector's inquiry," he said.

"What do you mean, Mr. Moncrieff?"

She offered, "What Hugh means is that he thinks Richard and I are having an affair."

"And you're not." I said.

"The very idea!" she shot back.

Moncrieff lowered his lids over his eyes, slumped in the chair, and mumbled.

"If there is nothing more, I'll be leaving," I said. "Please let me know should you decide to leave the county for any reason."

"Let me walk you out to your car, Chief Inspector."

At the car, Moncrieff proffered, "Something about Richard, from what I've heard, his property deals all failed miserably. He's been terribly unsuccessful freeing himself from dependence on Francesca's money. Never a

detail man. Never says anything, but his type always re-
sent relying on others."

"His type?

"The land-poor upper classes at middle age."

* * *

I went over to Pembroke in the evening, finding only one
of the servants about, a young maid named Mary, a rosy
cheeked, fair complexioned lass. Carlyle explained that
his wife was most keen on having staff live in the village, not at the Hall, but in the days after Francesca died
he'd been uncomfortable in the large house and proposed
someone might stay a week or two while he became accustomed to the quiet.

"Everyone begged off the duty, except young Mary
here."

I'd seen Mary around town and overheard my young
constables chatting about her. Last summer she'd blos-
somed. Noticeably. And her spending went more to lipstick
and eye liner than larger blouses. When Mary brought us
whiskey and sodas, Carlyle's following eyes, and her mincing step made me think there may have been more to
Mary's duties than answering the door and cleaning.

"One more thing before I go. The night of the party,
the Moncrieffs seem to think that your wife left first."

"Curious. I looked around and someone told me she was caught up in a game of bridge."

"I don't suppose you'd remember who told you?"

Carlyle cocked his head in a "no."

I walked toward the door, and as a last minute thought, asked, "Tell me, what were the relations between Mr. Moncrieff and your wife? Anything more than good neighbors?"

"I rather had suspicions of something going on between them."

"And you and Mrs. Moncrieff?"

"Really, Chief Inspector. You've been watching too much *Downton Abbey*."

Mary showed me to the door. As she opened it, I asked her, "We understand from the RSPB that they sent a letter by Royal Mail Sameday to Mrs. Carlyle the morning before she died. Did you see the letter in the post?"

"Well, Mr. Carlyle was there beside me when the post arrived and took it, actually he more like grabbed it from me hand, said he'd deliver it to Mrs. Carlyle." She reached for my hand, "Sir, about . . ." And then Carlyle called her from the library. "Later," she said, in an urgent whisper.

* * *

The next afternoon, when I walked into the station, Sergeant Sellman was typing up reports. "Albert, grab a cup of tea, one for me, and let's see where we are."

"So, who wanted her dead?"

"Her husband, so her money didn't go to the birds." Sellman knew me better than to add *literally*. "Add to that, the RSPB pledge form he claimed he knew nothing about, but did, having grabbed it from Mary."

Sellman looked back at his notes. "Then there's Sara Moncrieff, a rival for Carlyle's affections, who might have wanted her out of the way. And something I learned today. The boy at the stable said Mrs. Moncrieff's horse was there when he arrived early the morning after the murder. And there until she rode off, mid-day."

"Comforting the afflicted?"

Sellman laughed.

"She might have wanted retribution for the alleged affair between her husband and Mrs. Carlyle," I thought. "Or, welcomed an opportunity to switch husbands and enjoy Mrs. Carlyle's money. Hugh Moncrieff is a bully, in addition to being borderline alcoholic."

Sellman looked up at the ceiling and shook his head, "You know, sir, I don't understand these people, their affairs."

"Simple, my boy. Life can be quiet in the country. When us lot want a bit of fun, we go down to the pub for a pint or two. That lot, they go up to the bedroom for a shag."

"Both of them had an opportunity to smother her. Didn't take much, given her condition. But we haven't found the cushion or pillow used. Those we sent up to London for testing came back with only the servants' prints on them."

Frustrating this, suspects, motives, cause of death, no evidence.

"Albert, talk to Mary. Find out if she found anything amiss the next morning during her cleaning rounds."

"My pleasure, sir," with a broad smile.

"Not so fast. If you've noticed, and it's hard to believe you haven't, this young girl is aching to change her station. From my experience, there are two ways, the right way and the wrong way. She appears bent on the latter."

* * *

Sellman later reported that he'd found Mary at the chemist's. "May I ask you some questions about Mrs. Carlyle?"

"It'll cost ya a tea and scone."

They went to Bea's Tea Room. I know the place, cozy with lace curtains, butter yellow walls, and floral print chair covers. Mary said the day Mrs. Carlyle died, as every day, she counted the pillows on the chairs in the main salon and found one missing.

"Quite particular, was Mrs. Carlyle, didn't trust a soul.

Thought everybody was out to pinch something from her. Such a habit counting I had, even though she were a goner, I did it anyway."

"And did you find it?" Sellman said he nearly leaped across the table with hope.

Justified, when Mary said, "It was two days later, stuffed in the linen closet, of all places. So put it back where it belonged, didn't I? Now the others were brought back."

Sellman bribed Mary with another scone and she took him back to Pembroke to recover the pillow.

* * *

After the tests on the new-found pillow were in, Sellman and I drove out to Carlyle's house at the end of the day. No one answered our ring. We opened the door and went through the house into the garden. Carlyle was stretched out on a chaise with a drink, Mabel on his arm. He seemed to have found some peace with a creature he'd once blamed for changing his life-style. The setting sun ignited the yellow roses climbing the east wall. The remains of a cold plate and bottle of wine were on the table. A man at his ease. We watched him savor his last minutes of freedom. As the sun fell behind the wall, a murmuration of starlings traced wide circles in the evening sky.

Mabel sounded, "kak, kak, kak."

Carlyle removed Mabel's jesses from her legs and flung the bird into the sky. She climbed slowly, high above the starlings, wheeled, then dove and struck.

Lucia and Kevin

Bologna and New York, Recently

I scanned the foyer of the Opera House to avoid acquaintances. I wanted to be alone with *Elektra* this evening, as the day had been rather wretched. At the far end, in the corner, I saw a woman with short black hair and a pale thin face. I could hardly breathe as I pushed my way toward her. Her eyes, a haunting gray.

"Excuse me, my name is Lucia Fuoco. You look so like my dear friend Francesca, the resemblance is unearthly."

She backed away. "Well, I'm not Francesca."

"I know, but please, I didn't mean to be rude." I touched her arm. "It's just that, well . . . could we talk for a moment? Come, we'll be alone in my box."

When we sat down, she said, "Who is, or was, this Francesca?"

"We grew up together. Last week she was murdered. When I saw you, I thought she'd returned to earth. Alas, no." I took a picture of Francesca from my purse. "You see the resemblance, no? That is why I was overwhelmed."

The woman nodded.

"After the performance we might have dinner, and talk. Anyone who so looks like Francesca must be interesting."

She raised her eyebrows, in doubt, I think. Then, "Not late, I just flew in from Haifa. Oh, my name is Mia Allen."

"Piacere. Haifa, why did you go there?"

"A friend of mine, a man who saved my life, died there. He was badly injured on a mission in Iran. His sister said he asked for me. I flew over and was with him when he died."

I took Mia's hand. "I'm terribly sorry. We are both in mourning for our friends. You cannot forget a friend, you cannot replace a friend, but you can make a new friend."

She nodded, with hesitation. "Yes, you can try."

"Why did you come this evening?" I asked.

"I wanted to see this gorgeous Teatro Comunale. And I love the line in this opera 'When the right blood under the hatchet flows.' I can identify with it."

Blood. I can't stand blood. Ever since that afternoon.

The singing was splendid and the operatic deaths depressing. In that mood, we arrived at the restaurant, Drogheria della Rosa. Emanuele's greeting was effusive as always. He threw his arms around me and squeezed. That man is sexy, too bad about the wife and daughter.

"Caro, meet my new dear friend from New York."

"So charmed to meet you. Welcome to Bologna. This is your first visit?"

"Yes, but I feel I know it. A friend in business school never stopped talking about the torri, the pasta, and the portici."

Mia shared my love of good wine, long into the night. We told one another everything, though, I kept quiet about my early days as a dancer in London. Mia told me about life as una paladina, a lone warrior, tracking down alimony skips and guys who beat up on their wives. Then, how she served in the Israeli army pushing Palestinians back into their own territory. It was hard to picture someone the size of Mia in mountains and fields shooting people.

When we left the restaurant, Emanuale presented each of us with a blooming blood red rose, "Darlings, for you, and for you."

Outside the restaurant, I asked, "Where is your hotel? I will take you."

"Al Cappello Rosso."

"You cannot, you must not, that is where Giancarlo was killed. I will not let you stay there. You will come with me."

"Are you sure? I don't want to be trouble."

I couldn't tell if Mia was uncomfortable with my sudden affection or naturally shy. The whole evening had been so intense, a blur of images. I gave her the bedroom that looks out over the valley. A fluffy bed with soft linen sheets, fifteen foot ceilings and tall windows. She was half asleep when I peeked in twenty minutes later and padded across to her. She lifted her head.

"An old custom. When Francesca and I lived together in the convent, and in London, before we went to sleep, I would come to her bed and give her a kiss on the cheek."

In the dark, I missed her cheek and kissed her on the lips. She didn't pull back, nor did I. Instead, I held the kiss, made it longer and deeper, until she raised the sheet, took my hand and pulled me in. A frisson charged through us when our skin touched. Then Mia began a slow journey with her tongue, starting at my neck, licking my nipples, traveling down my stomach to the insides of my thighs. Followed by an explosion of joy, bittersweet, so like Francesca.

* * *

I was sitting at my desk in the 10th Precinct when my partner burst through the door.

"Yo, KFC, how's it going?" Murph crowed.

"How many times I gotta tell you I hate that?" My mother had worked for the Colonel. Actually, she fried chicken at the store in Astoria. And brought buckets home for dinner and lunch and dinner and…

"Not exactly like I'm gonna stop it now, Kevin Francis Connelly."

"Murph, we need to talk. I'm thinking we got a hell of a case on our hands. That guy, Danny O'Rourke, got shot some months back, one through the heart in the Park, coached in the Police Athletic League up on 119th? He wasn't the first vic shot with a rifle, at distance, recently."

Brendan Murphy flopped into a rickety wooden chair. Both he and the chair nearly collapsed. "Do tell."

"From the striations on the bullet, Ballistics established that it was fired from a sharpshooter rifle. Danny's killer used one with a five-groove rifling. A couple of months before, this diamond guy, a five-figure contributor to the Widows and Children's Fund, had his knee taken out by a sniper rifle. Got this from the guys over in the 72nd in Brooklyn."

"Been doing your homework, young man. Bucking for sergeant?"

I ignored the dig.

"Here it gets interesting, different striations, polygonal rifling, but this time we know the shooter was a lady."

"You're kidding. Diamonds ain't a girl's best friend?"

"The security guard at Green-Wood reported it. Happened just as the sun was setting. He saw it going down, but can't identify the shooter."

"What? He got scared and scampered away?"

"Better yet, when she turned around, she noticed him, then walked toward him, shucked her clothes as she closed in, unsnapped her bra, let it drop from her shoulder, and was in the process of slipping her panties off when he spooked and ran."

Murph leans forward in his chair. "Tell me he doesn't remember her face, her hair, or her shoes?"

"Right, only the bra and panties were red and she was stacked."

"If you're looking for help on the case and need someone to check out Vicky C's customer list . . . this I can do for you."

"Wouldn't put you out."

"Well, now it's narrowed down. Are we finished?"

"Not yet. It gets better. Couple months before, early morning, Asser Levy Park, Russian guy popped, one through the heart. And this time the shooter used a barrel with six right hand grooves."

"So we have one sniper using a different rifle for each job. Or, three snipers. I like the first option. But what do we got for motives? How do we tie these guys together—Danny the American investment banker, Isaac the Jewish jeweler, Sergei the Russian something?"

"Oh, we know what Sergei did," I said. "He was a pimp, big time."

"Huh?"

"Part of a sex traffic ring, FBI is following up on his associates. The Feds aren't too sorry about what happened to him, but like us, want to know who was behind his demise."

* * *

After the first night, Mia and I closed the door to the world. We were lost in the smell and touch of our bodies, the stories of our lives, the sheer pleasure of our encounter. Then, she had to get back to her business. And I went with her to New York, just for a while, we said. We took a taxi from the airport to her place on the upper West Side. It was nice enough, but it was clear she didn't spend a lot of time there. The sofa, mamma mia, an outsize lime and pink floral print that would ruin a beach house. The chairs were overstuffed and covered in fabric with faded green leaves. I'll redecorate while she's at work. Her electronics were non-existent. I'll install a Nest alarm and camera like I have, and Alexa. So convenient. That will be my thank you gift.

We went out to dinner the night after we arrived, a place called Rotisserie Georgette on east 60th. Style of Louis XV-meets-the-kitchen. We lounged in high backed chairs by the window.

"Tell me more about being a paladin with a detective's license."

"There was this guy running a sex trafficking business over in Brooklyn and . . ." We were interrupted when Georgette came over, welcomed Mia back and sat down with us. Turned out she was from Cannes, where Francesca and I had spent some time.

We walked back to Mia's place. "Lucia, did you notice anyone following us when we left the restaurant?"

"That, cara, is your line, not mine."

The next morning, she went off to work early. I went over to Verizon on Broadway to buy a new cell phone. I love American technology. I wanted one like Mia had, an iPhone 6. I spent the rest of the morning downloading apps: Lyft for taxis, Duolingo for when I forget a word in English, ColorSnap and Houzz for decorating, some just for women, like VithU and Nirbhaya.

I do not know if she put it in my head or not, but as I was shopping on Madison Avenue, I thought I saw a man, dark hair, glasses, gray slacks, and jacket, following me. In and out of stores I went. He was across the street, or down the block, or buying a paper at the kiosk on the corner. I came out the side door of Barneys, while he was watching the front door, I hailed a taxi. Mia came home an hour later, exhausted after her first day back at work. We dipped down to Santa Fe, a restaurant a couple of blocks from her place on 71st, for shrimp in flaky corn batter, tortilla soup, and margaritas.. I told her about the man.

Back at the apartment after dinner. Mia sat me down in a chair, went into the kitchen, and came back with two glasses and a bottle of Chianti.

"Lucia, I'm sure we are being followed. I may be the reason. There are a couple of things I haven't told you."

She leaned back in her chair, crossed her legs, relaxed. "I killed a man and crippled another one some months ago."
"You what?"

"Favors for the man who saved my life, the one whose funeral I went to."

"Favors?"

"Sergei ran an international sex trafficking ring. The Israeli government, and a few others, wanted to eliminate him."

"You had to kill him?" I leaned over and touched her knee.

Mia explained slowly, "It is so awfully difficult to get any of the girls to testify. They're afraid for their lives. So I had to kill him." She refilled our glasses.

"You had to do it?"

Mia sat up, her eyes darkening. "You're having a problem here?"

"I never thought it was easy to kill someone."

"It's not, but you have to put it out of your head."

"No, you know what I mean, you don't think about it afterward?"

"I can't. I wouldn't be any good if I did."

"There is no other way?"

"If there were, I would." Mia shoved herself out of the chair and went to bed. I did too, but couldn't sleep. Mia is so direct, so certain about everything.

The next night, Mia decided she needed to show me the lower East Side. One of her favorites, the Black Crescent. New Orleans Po'Boy sandwiches washed down with whiskey. We walked a couple of blocks after leaving the restaurant. Mia had been looking around every hundred meters or so. She saw him. It looked like the man who had followed us before. Same size, same jacket, same glasses.

"Lucia, we're going to get rid of him. Do what I say, no questions."

She took my hand and we hurried down a wide street, lots of light and cars. I thought we were near a river. The wind smelled of water. Then we walked under an elevated highway into a park.

"Mia! Is this right? We want to be in the dark?"

"Trust me. I know what I'm doing."

She dragged me through the grass to a railing overlooking a river and stopped.

"Now," Mia said, "Move over there, about two meters away from me."

The man walked slowly towards us, hands in his jacket pocket, but veering a bit toward Mia, then toward me, a little unsure who he wanted. In the dark, Mia and I look quite the same.

Mia whispered, "Get ready."

The man came closer. I could see the lights along the railing gleaming in his small eyes.

Mia called out, "Looking for someone, loser?"

Quickly, he pulled a knife from his pocket and ran toward Mia. She stepped to the side, grabbed his arm, and flipped him over the railing. We heard a scream and a splash. Looked down, he was flailing in the water. "I can't swim, I can't swim, help me."

Mia said, "It's time to go."

"And leave him?" I didn't see how we could leave someone who's drowning.

We turned around, two policemen, one on his walk-ie-talkie. The other pulled out a flashlight and shone it in the water. "Looks like he grabbed on to something."

Policeman on the walkie-talkie said, "Boat's on the way." Then turned to us. "I'm Officer Diaz, ladies, we've been following this guy for three blocks, saw him tailing you. Anything we ought to know about?"

"No," Mia said.

"Then why did you toss him in the river?"

"He scared us with a knife and we want to get rid of him," I said, a little more Italian accent than usual.

"Tell you what, we're all going to stay here until the boat fishes this guy out of the water and then the four of us will take a ride downtown to the station."

* * *

"Hey Murph, look at this, two dames, picked up last night in East River Park, tossed some smuck in the wa-ter. Diaz called me. I'd put out a call to be notified of any arrests of dames with guns. Didn't have guns, but one of the ladies is a private dick, American, the other visiting from Italy."

"So, the soaked-to-the-skin smuck was harassing them?"

"Not sure that's enough to put him in a hospital for three weeks."

"Whatever."

"But it gets more interesting, Diaz said the American dame was in the Israeli army, and quite an eyeful."

"And you are going to make a link to the sniper shootings in Brooklyn. Or, do you just want to take a look at them?"

In the interrogation room, the pixie-cut brunette in a red suit and white blouse and the long haired Italian dame in slacks, vest, and black tie, sat across the table from us. We switched on the light and the one called Miriam Allen leaned back in her chair. Her skirt rode up to mid-thigh. Good legs. The other dame, Lucia Fuoco, sat upright looking away. Allen's eyes said, *What's the game, boys? What do you have on us?*

"So ladies, what's your story about last night?" About walking into a dark park when someone was following you. Doesn't add up."

Fuoco spoke up first, "We already tell to other policemen last night. We tell again?"

"Yeah, again."

"This man, he follow me for two days. I scared. He so big. Then last night, to see river better, we lean over railing, he run at us with knife, I more scared, we push him and he fall. He all right?"

"Do you care?"

"We afraid."

"Cracked ribs, concussion, and a fractured wrist. Hit the embankment on the way over."

"He was a pig, un porco."

I could listen forever to this Italian dame with her accented and slightly broken English, but I was mostly interested in the other one.

"Miss Allen, what did you do in the Israeli army?"

"Quartermaster Corps, they figured somebody with an MBA ought to know how to move stuff around."

"Did you learn how to fire a gun?"

"Detective, you weren't in the military, were you?"

"No, why?"

"Those weapons with long barrels are called rifles."

"What's the difference?"

"Anyone's been in the Army knows 'one's for fighting, one's for fun.'" She cocked her head toward my crotch. Murph about fell out of his chair.

"Can we get back to the issue? Did you learn to fire a rifle?"

"Yes, but only in basic training. After that, once every six months the supply geeks went out for half a day and blasted away at some paper targets."

"Why did you go to Israel a month ago?"

"A friend of mine died."

"One more question, Miss Allen. Do the names Sergei Kasperov or Isaac Blum mean anything to you?"

"Should they?"

"Both were shot by a sniper. One died, the other lost his knee. Both had ties back to Israel. You have a license to carry?"

"A .38."

"That's all for now. Don't leave town, ladies."

When the women left the room, Murph chuckled, "Nice job, Romeo. All that preening. New tie and clean shirt. You were playing slow pitch soft ball."

"Let's say I was getting the lay of the land. Not a bad landscape. More homework to do, check out the Israeli angle, check out shooting ranges in the area, snipers gotta practice a lot. I was at the Academy with a guy who was so good he could knock an eye out at 500 feet. You do Israel, find out what she really did. Quartermaster unlikely, and check out that guy whose funeral she said she went to. What did he do? I'm going to take a trip to some of the local ranges."

"So, what time do you figure it is in Tel Aviv?"

* * *

Mia shook me awake. "Rise and shine, sweetheart, we're going shooting this morning."

"We are doing what?"

"I need to practice."

"Why? What we talked about. I thought maybe you weren't needing to."

"Come along, if only for the ride, keep me company, I'll show you some of the country, Hudson River Valley, prettiest in the US of A, late lunch at Brasserie 292."

"Va bene. I should see you, and with my new app I find you the quickest way." I did not want to encourage her, but did not know how to stop Mia from killing. She said we had to dress up like boys because we would stand out too much as women. I didn't know myself in the mirror: sports bra to smash my breasts a bit flat, red flannel shirt, boxer shorts even (if your pants slip, someone would notice lace, for sure, Mia said), baggy jeans, and hiking boots. No make-up, stocking cap over my eye brows. I did not like my look. My nose was a beak. When I came into the living room, Mia was kneeling by the side of the sofa, a rifle in her arms. She had a baseball cap with initials NY in white on backwards and a blue down vest. She made a cute ragazzo, someone I would go for.

"Is that where you keep the rifle?"

"Oh no, it's in a locked closet in my room." She stood up. "Now our names, you'll be Luke, I'm Mike. All the way up to the range, at the range, and at lunch."

She said her cover was as a kid, practicing to get into the Special Forces.

In the drive up the Hudson Valley we were in the foothills of Switzerland, but more dramatic with a winding wide blue river, green hills, mountains, stony cliffs down to the water, gardens. We got to the Wawarsing Gun Club and walked out to the 200-meter shooting range. The man in charge asked Mia/Mike, "You still trying, huh?"

"Yup," she said, low voice.

To me she murmured, "You take these binoculars. Tell me where the shots go."

She got ready slowly, went down on her stomach, spread her legs, laid her rifle in the crook of her left hand, rested her elbow just so on the ground, put the butt end into her shoulder. I saw her back rise, fall slightly, a ping, the target moved. She did that 100 times, but didn't hit the center black circle, not one time. When she took a break, I asked, "How can you shoot a person if you cannot come close to the middle?"

"I'm aiming at the edges."

"You are missing on purpose?"

"If they knew how good I was they'd get suspicious. This way they think I'm just a kid with lousy aim." Then she told me where she would hit on the stripes, then did. I thought she was a showoff but, "See the fluttering yellow leaf on the tall tree about 300 meters out." She shot. "Now do you see it?"

On the way back from the Gun Club, I tried asking her about this shooting of people she was doing.

She turned on me, "I don't like it, but somebody has to do it. Remember *Elektra*, 'When the right blood under the hatchet flows?' That's why."

"Is there no other way?"

"No, and let's drop it." She ripped off her baseball cap and flung it in the back seat. "Okay?"

* * *

Murph came through the door beaming. "How's this? The guy whose funeral she went to. There was a picture in the Haifa paper *Arutz Sheva*. Guess who else was there?"

I shook my head.

"The head of Mossad. And this dame wanted us to believe she trucked backpacks and matzo balls around the country for the troops?"

"Me. I went up to The Pub last night. Place where O'Rourke hung out. Bartender told me he saw our Miriam Allen with him more than once in the last six months. Plus, Danny told him a while back, before he was shot obviously, they were seeing one another."

The shooting range angle didn't work out. No one fitting the description. They said if a dame, especially a looker came out regularly, they'd notice. Only non-hunter/non-skeet shooters out on Staten Island were young guys, mostly lousy shots. Couple of them said they wanted to join the SEALS.

"Murph, here's what I'm thinking. With the Israeli army connection, the funeral of a Mossad guy, and the link to the Pub, we might, just might, convince a judge to grant a search warrant."

* * *

While Mia worked, I spent the day throwing out her tatty furniture and arranging the new things I'd bought at ABC Carpet. At about six o'clock she burst through the door and shrieked, "What the hell is going on?"

"Cara, your salon, you furnished it from your grandmother's house?"

"The sofa? Where's my fucking sofa?"

"That falling apart bamboo thing, so uncomfortable. St Vincent de Paul took it away."

"You didn't even fucking ask me? That sofa was . . . important."

Before I could explain, there was pounding and shouting at the door.

"Police, open up."

"What the fuck!" Mia shouted back, but opened the door.

Detectives Murphy and Connelly, the ones we talked to at the police station, barged in. "We have a warrant to search this apartment in connection with the deaths of Daniel O'Rourke, Sergei Kasperov, and an assault on Isaac Blum. When we finish, we are going to your office on 43rd Street."

"Be my guest, officers. Lucia, come into the kitchen. We could use a drink."

One of the uniformed cops shouted out, "Hey Detective, a .38 in this drawer."

"She's got a license for a pistol. It's not what we're looking for."

A lot of shouting. I peeked out of the kitchen door.

They were pulling out drawers and throwing things on the floor. The carabinieri are not this way. Much more respectful of the home.

"Nothing in the dresser but clothes and a department store collection of lingerie," one of the cops said.

"Anything red?"

"No, but black and white and pink and … you want me to go on?"

* * *

Back at the precinct, I paced up and down, throwing files, phones, papers, "Goddam it to hell! Where does she keep those guns? We checked banks, safe deposit boxes, storage facilities, in Manhattan and Brooklyn. We ain't got a case without one of those guns."

"Rifles," Murph reminded me.

"Go to hell!" The warrant had been a stretch, a favor. No more fishing.

"We ever find out the name of that guy that went over the railing?" Murph asked.

"Some Dmitri Askov, a Ukrainian with a British passport, who, by the way, is not pressing charges against the women for reasons he's unwilling to explain."

Murph added, "And denies ever having a knife."

* * *

After the police left, Mia poured another drink. "We'll call St. Vincent de Paul first thing in the morning and collect the sofa. Did they say where they were taking it?"

"Queens? Is there a Queens?"

"The pieces of my rifles were in the sofa. The barrels were in the bamboo support pieces I hollowed out, the rest of the rifle was in the cushions. If you hadn't redecorated, I don't know what would have happened. Oh, you lovely, lovely inspired creature."

She put her arms around me and kissed me. When the kiss finally finished, she slumped against me and her eyes were wet. "What am I going to do now? I can't protect women against being assaulted."

I sat her down on the sofa and took her hands. "You know I never liked what you did, so I've been thinking about other ways to protect women. Maybe we can work on developing an app to protect women.

"Do what?"

"While you were working, I downloaded apps and investigated them. There is one used in colleges in California called Callisto. It matches complaints against men by different women. NextDoor lets people report suspicious activity in their neighborhood, and LiveSafe has a button that calls the police and tells them where you are."

I hadn't quite figured out how to make sure only

women could subscribe to the app, but thought there must be a way.

"That's a marvelous idea, Lucia. You are truly a woman of many, many talents. And I know people who can help us. People I went to school with are in tech and venture capital."

* * *

"Yo, KFC, remember those dames we had in here, what was it, six months ago? The Italian and the sniper. You see the *News* this morning?"

I looked up. Murph had an announcement every morning. Most times, the newest way the Knicks or Giants managed to lose. "Yeah."

"They're famous. Press conference with the Chief and Mayor about this app "Hands Off" they developed to protect women from scummy guys. Been testing it on the West Side for a couple of months. Nailed five creeps so far, all awaiting trial."

"Good thing we didn't find the red panties."

Down at the Devil

Up there on stage, she was singing

I heard that shrieking whistle blow,
Mean, hard and screaming low,
Lying in my cold, cold bed,

About there, she stopped, swallowed hard and squeezed her eyes. Wasn't sure she'd get to the next lines. But took a deep breath, leaned into the mike and finished up with

Wrapped round my darling,
My darling dear dead Fred.

Sent shivers through me. Girl twisted around a dead guy.

Olivia Hart was the new act at the Red Devil Lounge. Dark brown hair, skin pale in the stage lights; slim, still on her way to becoming a woman. Could kind of tell from how she moved. Like she wanted to be sexy, but ended up angles. Nice voice, bit of huskiness to it.

She ended her set with *Travelin' Soldier* then slipped off behind the stage. Never came out front afterwards like most performers do. Hoping she would. Wanted to ask her about that song.

Asked Jake about her. He yanked the dirty rag from his left shoulder, wiped down the bar, settled it back, shrugged. "She showed up one afternoon and said she could sing and play. Did *Fire and Smoke*. The boss liked her and hired her on."

The Devil is in a cutout in the woods along Veteran's Highway, a bit south of Baltimore. Flaking white building in the middle of a parking lot, fading red neon outline of a devil hanging off the roof. Inside, it's always night. Dim yellow bulbs draped over wooden booths. A small stage at one end. A place like a lot of others I've been in. Marsh nearby gives it a swampy feel.

Next morning I was down behind the counter at the lumberyard. Couldn't get 'dear dead Fred' out of my mind. Tune buzzed in my brain. What's it like for the girl? The guy's not breathing, but she doesn't want to move, hoping something, anything, waiting for a twitch, an eye to open. Falls asleep, hurdles down a coal mine 'til the light at the top of the shaft is only the wink of a faraway star. Screams herself awake, a stiff body beside her.

Wanted to know if this was for real. So, at eight

o'clock I was down at the Devil for the first set. Olivia came on stage in a bright yellow satiny blouse and big silver hoop earrings. Led off with the song about Fred.

"This is about what happened to a girlfriend of mine."

After, I went over to Jake. "Like to talk to Olivia. Tell her I'll buy her a drink, whatever, I want to find out about this dead guy."

"Anything for a pal." He winked, like I had other things on my mind.

When she finished the set, Jake motioned to her, and she came over. He leaned over the bar, nodded in my direction. She turned away, whispered something. He put his hand on her arm, shook his head, like, "He's okay."

I stood up, put out my hand. "Hi, name's Greg Lizer. I'm real curious, that song about Fred. Buy you something?"

"Well, haven't eaten all day, hear they have good steak. You up for something like that?"

Not what I had in mind, but out of the glary stage lights, she was more than just a little pretty… high cheeks, maybe some Indian in her.

She slid into the booth. "So, what do you want to know?"

"That business about a girl wrapped around a corpse, it's haunting me."

"Can't say it didn't happen."

"Who's this Fred?"

"Soldier who come back home."

I got short answers like that. Seems she didn't want to talk much about the song. Least not to a stranger.

I bought her another beer to go with the steak and she started on talking about herself. Growing up in Martinsburg, West Virginia. Small town, about fifteen thousand, and getting smaller with people leaving, nothing to do, no jobs. What with the wars it seemed like every guy she went to high school with, plus a few of the girls, left for Iraq or Afghanistan, at least once. She'd hung around for a while – clerk at Wal-Mart, classes at Mountain State College.

"Mamaw taught me how to play guitar when I was little. Not 'til I finished high school did I take it up for real. Some gigs now and again in small towns — Sharpsburg, Hagerstown.

All the while she's telling me this, she's playing with her napkin, tearing it into little snowflakes.

"So your friends who went off. What happened?"

"A bunch never came back. Michelle's Fred did. Least ways, the body part of him. What she said, one night Fred's squad was in their tent, an IED was thrown in. He was the only survivor."

Knew what that was like. We've got a fellow down at work, feels guilty all the time because he made it back.

"Michelle would look at him while he was asleep. Said she remembered what he was like deep down, before. Then Fred'd wake up frightened, thrash around, flailing, hit her sometimes. She'd have to hold him to squeeze out the demons. Did that for him, even when he was begging 'let me go, I want to go.'"

Olivia shuddered, shook her head. "You should've seen her morning after. Terrible. Hardly hold herself together. Took half her tables at the diner we were working."

"Couldn't he go to the VA there?"

"The VA drugs he got only made him mean. Michelle helped him mellow out with the street variety."

Leaned across the table to catch everything she was saying. She's leaning too, so's our heads were near to touching. Here in the booth, she wasn't up on stage performing, just being lonely.

Seemed we'd been talking a couple of hours, a loud noise at the bar; some yahoo took a poke at a guy, and bottles started flying.

"Excuse me, Olivia, I've got to go give Jake a hand here."

Not that he couldn't have handled it himself. Ex-linebacker, face carved with a hatchet, played for the Ravens a couple of years, before that starred at Rutgers. Him and me settled them down, tossed two guys into the parking lot. They're still picking gravel out of their butts. When I came back, Olivia'd gone. Figured I might as well get on home. Cooper, my golden lab, would be wanting his walk.

Next night I was back at the Devil, walked in, got hit by the damp funk. Heavy fog made it worse. Olivia's not there. Jake said she called in sick. My face must have showed something.

"You getting hooked, buddy?"

"Worried a bit about her. A sweet gal, still finding herself out here in Millersville."

I was feeling on the edge between an older brother and something else, though probably a good fifteen years between us. Jake didn't say anything, smiled, and nodded.

Friday night, word had gotten around. The place was packed. Even after three sets, the crowd wouldn't let her go, kept throwing money into the hat on stage. Made my way up front, gave her a hug, told her she'd done swell and left her to her new fans.

Saturday's a busy day at the lumberyard. Bunch of do-it-yourselfers. Tell me what they're trying to do. I work up the measurements and suggest the type of wood they'll need. Enjoy that. I did my own place. Started when I moved in. Took a couple of years, but now every room is different, lots of hand carving. Butternut cabinets in the kitchen, dark swirly sassafras floors in the living room. That Saturday, didn't finish 'til after ten and I was bushed, went home.

The Devil's closed on Monday, but Tuesday evening I got there early. Olivia was having a coke at the bar. Different, way she perched there. More confident like. She saw me, slipped off the stool, gave me a big wide smile, looked me in the eye, first time for that, and took my hand. First time in a while for a little female affection. I'd been breathing the ashes from the last lady for a bit.

"Hear you're a star hereabouts now," I grinned.

She blushed a little, looked down. "Good crowd here Saturday night. Couple of people said guy at a lumberyard told them about me. That you?"

"Might a-been. See you after? Dinner?"

She smiled a "yes."

She was a bit more comfortable tonight up on stage. Patter between songs. Guess it was the weekend crowds. No happiness like having people appreciate what you're doing.

We ended up eating at the Devil. After she finished off the steak, "One night Fred is real quiet, been that way for a week. Michelle's waiting for something. Sure enough, they're lying in bed, she and Fred, he started having a fit, hit her up side the head, she grabbed him, wrapped her legs and arms around him, held tight. He's screaming, "*Fire, Fire, Fire.*"

The last *fire* caught in her throat. She shut her eyes, closed down her face, squeezed herself, so's her blouse was near ripping. I got up, pushed in her side of the booth and put my arm around her. Good ten minutes before she stopped shaking and relaxed some. I sat there, didn't try to talk, holding on.

"I kept on squeezing, he fought back. Then a noise inside him and he went all limp. He jerked, then nothing. All night I held on. Friend come by to pick me up for work next morning and had to pry me off. He'd gone cold."

I think that was her moment. She got some calmness, some lightness, maybe freedom from the telling. Didn't sing that song again.

A couple days later, standing up there, outfit I hadn't seen before, pretty light blue dress matched her eyes, wide gold belt.

"Something new I've been working on, somebody special out there, he knows who he is, I reckon."

Love was a stranger who listened,
Could tell I had something to say,
Let me ramble on wherever I wanted,
Is how I'm a bit over it today.

Glad the lights were down. My face was too pink to face anyone. Over at the bar, Jake grinned wide.

Three weeks now, Olivia'd been here. Packing them in, during the week too. Owner took a while, but finally realized he had something and signed her up for three months. Bumped her money up too.

Sitting together after one of her sets, "Greg, I'm a bit tired of that motel down the pike. Never know from night to night who'll be next door. TVs blaring, people fighting, sometimes 'til dawn."

"You try talking to the owner?"

"Guess it's been a while since you've been in one of these places."

Confessed it might have been ten years.

"You know if there's an apartment around here I could rent for three/four months? Place with a kitchen, place with a bit of quiet. I'm getting frazzly."

Said I'd look around, ask down at the yard. But got to thinking. I had an extra bedroom at my place, its own bathroom, she worked nights, I mainly worked days, she'd have the run of the place. Would be nice to have the company. But, what would she think, taking advantage, a bit of a stretch from having dinner together, didn't know, but figured I wouldn't lest I asked her. I did, she said yes, and I got a kiss for the idea.

"But you'd have to share the place with my golden lab," I said.

"My best friend from first grade to high school was a chocolate lab. Rocket, cuz he used to chase off after cars."

Only thing we squabbled over was the rent. I said no, she said yes, we decided to settle it later.

Worked out pretty much the way I figured with her there days, me there nights. Sometimes she had some dinner ready. Not much of a cook, but tried hard. Even fried chicken, you'd of thought it was in mother's milk in these parts, eluded her.

After she went off to the Devil, I'd read, watch some TV, go to bed, but found I was staying awake 'til she got in. That's when Cooper got up from the bottom of my bed and went to her room. Couple of weeks after Olivia moved in, Cooper's split affections got sorted out. One night, heard the front door open, she seemed to be moving around more than usual, doors opening and closing, then footsteps near my bedroom. Backlit by the hall light, she stood there, in a long, man's shirt, bare feet.

"Can I come in?" A soft whisper.

I didn't expect this. Not that I never thought of it, or never wanted it to happen. "Yes," I said and held the blanket open for her. She undid the top buttons and the shirt fell to the floor. A pale thin shadow glided into my bed. She was warm, her skin electric on mine. It had been some time for both of us. In the morning, cradled in my arms, she had tears in her eyes.

"What's this?"

"This is happy. I was afraid I'd have bad memories, but I didn't."

Couple of weeks later, instead of slipping in beside me, she turned the bedside light on and sat up against the headboard, shadows playing off her honey soft breasts.

"Can we talk? Everything's going so fast, the music, me and you, it's beginning to get to me how this kind of life feels, the same club night after night, having a man, and a place to come home to. Thank you."

She reached over and gave me a long squishy kiss that would've lasted a lot longer, but I'd been thinking too, and now was as good a time as any. I pushed her away a little, so's I could look her straight in the eyes.

"Olivia, women like you are rare." She shook her head. "You are. Since I met you, the very first time even, been thinking again about the future. Not looking back."

"Something happen before?"

"That's for another time."

She put her hands around my head, like to comfort me even though she didn't know why.

"Now turn off the light, sugar."

"Okay," she said. "Not going to need light where we're going."

I'd remember that line, and that night.

Month went by, one night she came home after two in the morning and bounced into bed. I could feel a buzz in her body. "You'll never guess who came in tonight, Jesse Clemens, one of the best arrangers on the whole East Coast. Plus, he's done backup for Taylor Swift and Jana Kramer. And he likes my songs, what I'm doing. Offered to work with me."

"That's great news. But is he going to stick around? This is not exactly country music central."

"He's in Baltimore a couple of weeks. We'll see what we can do with my material."

"That's super, honey. A monster break."

But all I could feel breaking was my heart. I'm not stupid, I knew this was going to happen. She's young, has a future, wouldn't want to be tied down in this place for long, with a lumberyard guy. She got up three or four times during the night.

"You okay?"

"I'm fine, sometimes I get ideas and need to write them down before I forget them."

In the morning, she was there at the kitchen table. Fixed me eggs, bacon, and toast. Toast a little burnt.

"Wanted to tell you I might be getting in late for the next couple of weeks. Jesse works most of the day and the only free time together would be after my show. Jake said he'd let me have a key so we could work at the Devil long as we wanted. But what I mean ..."

"I think I can figure. You're going to be coming back here late and tired and needing sleep."

Hadn't been to the Devil for a month or so, let Olivia and Jesse have their time. Hell, might as well admit, I was jealous. Then Olivia asked me to come down and hear what she and Jesse'd done with her songs. Sweet gesture I thought, her leading off with *Love is a Stranger*. Hardly recognized it. The new arrangement speeded up the beat, created a different, almost cheerful feel. They added a guitar solo in the middle and wrote in a chorus.

> *Love is a stranger who listens,*
> *A stranger that cares about you,*
> *Just listens, no suppositions,*
> *Anytime I'm feeling down 'n blue.*

Jesse left for Nashville and Olivia's schedule got back to what it had been. But one Friday night, she was there to meet me at the door when I got off work. She'd gotten a call.

"The tracks we recorded with the new arrangements, Jesse played them for people at Big Machine, Taylor Swift's label."

"They want you to come down."

She tilted her head to the side, but not with the smile I expected to see, "Yeah."

I threw my arms around her. "This is major. You're on your way." Squeezed a couple of more times.

She kinda pulled away, wrinkled her forehead, "I don't know."

Why you hesitating?"

"I feel home here. You, this place, the Devil, first time in what seems forever."

She scooted herself up on my lap.

"That's sweet, Olivia, but you're too young to settle down, 'specially here."

"But you've here and here's where I'm safe."

I put her a little at arms' length, like giving her a lesson.

"Think about this. You give Nashville a try, a good try. Like in baseball you're not out 'til you miss three times."

"Could I come back?"

"If you want to." Doubted that would happen though.

"Nashville is big, maybe too, it might not be the right place, all those lights, all those people. I need time to think."

I never asked her what she was thinking, knew she was, way she tossed in bed. A week later, I walked in after work, there's two glasses and a bottle of bubbly on the table in the living room.

"You've been a real friend. A gorgeous man the like of what I'll never see again, only if I'm blessed by the Lord beyond all measure."

She was leaving. We sipped the champagne, she got teary, me too. In the morning, I took her to the airport. Driving back, thinking, that's the last I'll see her. But she didn't leave. At the house, I saw her shadow in the doorway, smelled her in bed. Cooper was worse off. Laid around, looked at me with those liquid brown eyes. *Your fault she's gone.*

Month went by, then an e-mail with a link to a video, the first track on her album.

"They glammed me up," she warned, "So much I hardly see me in the mirror."

But they didn't hide the blue eyes and the song was the one she wrote for me. Next week, another e-mail, "Watch CMT at 9 tomorrow. I'm on Grand Ole Opry. Do you believe? Wish you were here."

The MC came out to flashing red and yellow lights. "And now put your hands together for a lady you're going to be hearing a lot more from, Olivia Hart. And her new single from Big Machine: *Livin' with a Mean Man.*

She came out in a shimmery tight white gown.

He'd been a good one
That was once upon a time

War, drugs and whiskey
Turned him all around
Once huggin' lovin' arms
Now bruised my head and mind

End of the song the women in the audience jumped up clapping, guess they identified, kept her on stage, seemed five minutes.

Have to say, time's played funny tricks on me last couple of weeks, can't keep track, but I think it was afternoon, I was helping a mother, woman about my age, and her two little girls They wanted school desks. Ones they drew up themselves, measured out best they could. Kind of a sucker for this, and didn't hurt that the mother and girls were pixies with black hair and matching red tops and pants. I was in the middle of firming up the specs, boss taps me on the shoulder,

"You got a call. Guy on the line says it's important."

It was Jake. "Buddy, you better come down here now."

"I'm in the middle of helping some people.

"Now."

"Ms. Blair, I'll cut the wood, drill the screw holes, bring everything over tonight. You home?"

Down at the Devil, a bottle of whiskey and Jake were waiting for me at a corner table. His half-shut eyes told me we weren't here to celebrate. "Sit down, hombre."

"Why the mystery?"

"The cops were in here today. They want to talk to you.

Olivia's been arrested for killing a guy named Rusty Taylor in Martinsburg, six months ago."

I shook my head. Jake said it again. "Just before she showed up here."

I kind of got what he was saying the second time, least I understood the words, not that I believed any of them.

"Olivia and Rusty were living together. From time to time she'd move out. She couldn't stand his craziness full time. That, and he clubbed her a couple of times."

I didn't find that real hard to believe, what I'd read about PTSD and what she told me.

"They found him dead, but the cops couldn't find her anywhere. For a reason. She wasn't Olivia Hart. Her name was Sally French and Sally French was a blonde. And, no one knew she played guitar."

"What?"

"And the local medical officer couldn't figure how Rusty died."

"OD'd probably."

"That's the track they started down. And it took a while because the VA didn't want to release the list of what they were giving him."

"Like some experimental shit?"

"Didn't say. Police had to go to court to get the list. But none of that killed him."

"Huh?"

Jake's boss came out of the back. "Hey, you forget

we've got a private function tonight that starts in half an hour?"

"Sure. I got that. Just a bit more to do."

Jake got up, told me the party would keep him busy 'til two, but he'd meet me in the a.m. at Sadie's.

"Sorry buddy."

Left the Devil staggering with booze and the news. Drove around, didn't want to settle. Olivia, she loved that guy. That was clear from the day I met her. How could she end up killing him? How could she kill anyone?

Without meaning to, ended up back at the yard, looked for the drawings of the desks. Hell, I'd assemble them for the girls. Give me something to do. Called Ms. Blair, said I could be over tomorrow night.

Brought everything back to my shop in my garage. Went slow putting the desks together. Seen too many guys in the wood business with short fingers. And slow to keep me from thinking about Olivia. Not that it worked real well. Kept trying to understand what really happened and what she told me. Why I didn't see something. Hadn't been looking I guess, my head wasn't exactly leading the way.

Jake was at Sadie's early. "What killed Rusty was an embolism."

Shook my head. Never heard of that.

"An air bubble in his artery. Then they re-examined all the syringes they found. Two never had anything in them, but had Olivia's prints on them."

"They lived together."

"The cops figured she shot air into his veins."

"And that'll kill you?"

Jake nodded. "Sometimes. Usually takes a lot of air, but Rusty had a hole between the chambers of his heart. All it took was a little."

He stopped there, looked away. Gave me space to absorb what he was saying.

"When all this happened, the cops said Olivia was staying with a girlfriend. One day she went over to the apartment she and Rusty shared. He was passed out. Their dogs had been shot, pistol right there. That didn't figure, silver Labradors, his pride. She got scared what he'd do next. At least that's what the girlfriend told the cops."

"Something in him must of snapped. Her song, the first one, that's what it was about." I told Jake.

Put my head down on the counter, seemed like a few seconds.

Then Jake was shaking me. "You still with me?"

"They know dead certain it was Olivia?"

"She confessed. Said she did it for him. Said it's what he wanted."

"Sweet Jesus, pray for her."

Jake gave me a punch on the arm.

"A narrow miss there, buddy."

Not sure about that.

Storm Painter

The last time he saw her, she was crying, huddled in a corner of her apartment.

Today, she strode into the reception at the Algonquin in a short black sheath. Not the usual attendee at a party debuting a historical novel. He gasped. *What's she doing here?* She walked up to him, kissed him on both cheeks. He opened his mouth, nothing came out.

"I missed you at the bookstore so I dropped by to get your autograph."

He took the book, thankful for the minute to clear his head. *To Maggie, an inspiration. Michael.* Then he grinned. "You look good, what are you doing these days?"

"I paint storms. Lightning flashing, thunder pealing, purple, green, and gray skies. You must have seen Turner's *Snow Storm*, rocking black waves, swirling Prussian blue skies, a white sail flashing distress between them."

"Sounds magnificent. My cabin is in the middle of a

thunderhead every time there's a storm. You should stop in if you're ever in the area."

"Maybe I will. Good crowd tonight. Bye now."

Michael's agent came up to him. "You know Veneto? Why didn't you tell me?"

"What's the deal?"

"It's only that she's the hottest thing in the city. Those huge paintings she does. And she is absolute-ly stun-ning."

* * *

Four years earlier, Central Park. Michael saw a pretty girl sitting on a bench, sketching wildflowers. Twice he'd walked by and she was there. He stopped, com-plimented her on the drawings. But his usual flirt—friendly, not forward—didn't induce her to put down the drawing pad. The next time he saw her he decided to introduce himself, ask her name. He practiced his line, but when it came time to talk, stuttered. Maggie was shy, but he learned that she had been in New York a month since finishing an art program in Portland in the spring of '65. She had a part time job with the Mu-seum of Natural History sketching plants in the Park. Not her heart's desire, but it paid the rent. She want-ed to do a series of paintings that captured the cold of white moonlight and the slash of branches swayed by heavy winds.

"When someone sees my painting, I want them to physically shake and shiver." She wrapped her arms around her chest.

He looked at his watch. "Well then, we need to give you some strength. I'm hungry, you?"

"I usually don't eat until supper."

"Artists should be fed. Something I know about." He wanted her to ask how, tell her about life as a doctoral student in medieval history, followed by one as a struggling writer with crummy jobs—copy editor, janitor, tour guide. She didn't ask. They trudged the upper West Side past restaurants he knew from his time at Columbia. She hung a little behind, clutching her sketch pad to her chest. It was after three, so many places had closed for lunch. Finally, Noche Mexicana on Amsterdam. Dark wooden tables and paper napkins and the food as good as he remembered.

She asked about the book he was carrying. "Hey, that's you." She grinned at the picture on the back flap.

"Yup, my first, out three months. I was taking it to a friend."

"Congratulations, you must be happy."

"Relieved. I wrote two that never saw the light of day."

Maggie picked up the book. "From the cover, it looks like a historical novel."

"Yup."

"I've always kinda wondered, how do you do the people in your books? How do you make these people who lived so long ago real?"

"I research the characters and try to relate them to someone I know. That way I get some blood in their veins."

"Don't your friends find that creepy?"

"Nobody's said anything, yet."

She grabbed his arm. "You cannot use me, ever, never. You must promise."

"Easy, ma'am. I promise, cross my heart." He made a big show of crossing his heart, did it twice.

"I've got to go now." Michael had a meeting with his agent. *The Pillars of Chartres* received strong reviews and more importantly, the publisher made money three months after the book hit the shelves. He had the outline and one chapter of the next one, *The Mistress of Tours*. His agent and publisher were talking about a two-book deal. He hoped to sign before going back to his cabin in Vermont.

"Will you be by the Loch again? I'll come by if you are." He took her hand, softer and warmer than when she'd admonished him.

"I'd like that."

Some days later, sitting together in the Park while she worked, Maggie asked, "My place, tomorrow night? I make pretty good eggplant lasagna."

He found her apartment down on Avenue B. Rang

the bell. No answer. Up and down the street, kids tossed a baseball and people walked their dogs. He sat on the stoop. Kept looking at his watch — 10 after, 15 after, half past. Someone running.

"I am so, so sorry. I don't know what happened to the time. I just went to the corner to pick up some lettuce and Mr. Bezdikian insisted on telling me about his nephew he wants me to meet. Dinner's nearly ready."

"I had a late lunch." He hadn't. The wait was forgotten, noticing only her cropped black hair askew, a pink tint on her cheeks from the run, and a blue sweater matted to her.

Her studio was furnished with stacked canvases, easels, posters of Raphael's St Cecilia and Millais's St. Joan of Arc tacked on the wall, a mattress off to the side, and books. For dinner, they sat on the floor and used a suitcase for a table. The pasta was as good as promised.

He wanted to know about her attraction to saints in a state of ecstasy suffering gruesome fates. Instead, she got him talking about Paris, his room in the Latin Quarter, museums, crepes and croissants. He rambled on, especially to a rapt audience. He'd wanted to teach, but the demand for history profs specializing in medieval France, never high, was non-existent in the sixties. It didn't stop him from dressing like an East Coast academic, chinos, a blue button down shirt, and a tweed jacket with the mandatory leather patches. Maggie rested her elbows on the suitcase, kept her eyes on him as he waved his arms, dropped a few French phrases, and told about how he stumbled up the first step of the grand stairway when he looked up and saw Winged Victory.

After her second yawn, he looked at his watch, nearly midnight. "Time to let you get to bed. I don't want to wear out my welcome."

"If you're in the Park, I'll be near Springbanks Arch, at the north end. It has an iron railing."

He reached down, lifted her up and kissed her on each cheek.

In the days that followed, more meetings in the Park, more meals together. One night, after a dinner of clams and linguine at Umberto's on Mulberry, he walked her home.

"Can you come in?"

She turned on a small light by the door. Her apartment had a different feel. Neat, draped, uncluttered, and the mattress had been moved out from the corner of the room.

"Sit here."

She motioned to the chair furthest from the bed. She went into the bathroom. He heard her moving around. Five minutes later she emerged in a long shimmering tunic and stood beside the mattress.

"Come to bed."

He'd been careful not to push, he'd waited. She was fifteen years younger. Anticipation, the theme of great literature was, he knew, very seductive. He undressed and lay on the bed while she watched. She pulled on the bow at her neck, the tunic puddled on the floor, she stepped out of it, and knelt. They reached out, fingers on arms, on shoulders, slowly, as if their skin might burn from the touch, then sank into one another. She pulled him on top and opened to him. Every night was at her place, and sex was slow and tender. He made notes in his journal—*the low humming sound she made when he kissed her breasts, the earthy taste of her skin*—he might use these to describe one of his characters.

Two days before he was due to leave, he came back to her apartment in the afternoon and found her wrapped in sheets, bunched in the corner.

"It's no use. Why did I think I could be an artist? Look at this shit."

Shredded charcoal sketches lay in a pile around her. Portraits. One of him and some other people he'd seen in the park.

"They're good. You capture character in the faces."

"Sure, and you can buy the same thing for two dollars in Times Square."

He tried to cheer her, comparing her sketches to Durer and Rembrandt.

"You know nothing about art."

He sat in the corner beside her and held her hand. In the morning, he woke up to a face with large black circles for eyes. When he started to say something, she buried her head in the wall. He made tea and toast, set them beside her before going out. That evening, the apartment filled with candle light and the smells of tomato sauce. She wore a flowery print dress, the first time he'd seen her in one.

"I'm sorry. These bouts of depression, I don't know when they're going to happen."

* * *

His place in Vermont was ten miles from the village, down a packed dirt road. When he pulled in, a full moon washed the roof, lighting it like a borealis. The cabin sat near the bottom of a swale, a stream burbled below. Built of logs with tendon corners, its small white framed windows peered into the forest. The solitude allowed Michael to dream and create the worlds for his novels. He'd tried the city, but the clamor pummeled his focus. He wrote *Pillars* in this cabin. It became his talisman. If his next book was as successful as the first, he'd be able to make a down payment. Not that the cabin was large, but it sat on one hundred acres of land. The elderly couple who owned wanted to sell. They liked Michael and understood his situation, but made it clear they couldn't wait long.

* * *

A month later he came back to the city and stayed with Maggie. She woke him up one morning with, "I'd love a blue-eyed baby that looks like you."

"Maybe someday, but definitely not now."

She pulled back, clouds crossed her face.

The next time he visited her apartment, the smell of turpentine assaulted his nose. Maggie had begun to paint winter scenes. He thought she'd gotten the effect she was looking for, especially in a painting of snow laden pine trees and their reflection off the surface of a black lake. Eight four-by-six foot paintings lined the walls.

"I ran into a fellow who was in my French Lit class up on the East Side. He works at a gallery on Madison, family business. Couldn't make a go of it in academia," he said. "Can I bring him by?"

"It's much too soon. I'm only starting."

"Here's his name and phone number when you're ready, but I'm going to talk to him anyway about what you're doing."

Now that Michael was coming back every month, he noticed bulletins from St. Brigid's Church sitting on the kitchen counter. There was a six o'clock mass every morning. That explained the coffee, tea, and pastries she produced at seven.

* * *

Early October, six months after they'd first met, leaning into one another by the door as he was leaving. "I was wondering, do you think living with me up in the woods would give you scope for your painting?"

"As long as there are seasons, the sun rises and sets, and you are there, I'll have everything I want," she sang, threw her arms around him and nestled her head into the crook of his neck.

"I know it didn't sound like it, but this is a marriage proposal. Are you sure?"

"Yes, a thousand times yes."

* * *

Back in Vermont, hunched over his typewriter, he'd look out the window and see Maggie. Imagine her squeals of delight when he surprised her with flowers. Feel the lushness and eagerness of her body. He conjured them nesting in the cabin. He writing, she painting. He'd build a studio off to the side for her. He liked the idea of an artist nearby. Maybe he'd get a better feel about how to describe physical settings.

They'd walk in the woods. From a high point, he'd show her how trees moved in the wind. The white birch swaying, the stately hemlock hardly acknowledging the air. At night, they'd linger over a bottle of wine and console one another about what hadn't gone right. Every couple of months they'd go to New York for a week. And there would be her openings and his new books. Of course he'd give her a tour of Paris.

Lately, life had not been rolling out that way. Her depressions. She'd had one every time he visited the last four months. Her voice became faint and raspy, she ate nothing, had no interest in sex. The last time she stayed in bed for 48 hours.

"Maggie, it's a gorgeous day. We'll go to the park, have lunch at that new restaurant in the West Village, and the Morgan has a new exhibit,"

"So, you want to show me how awful my work is by taking me to a museum? Thanks. Now go away. I don't want to see you."

"What about the park and restaurant then?"

"Leave me alone, please, please."

It sucked his energy being with her during these moody periods. He didn't understand why they happened or what to do when they did. Once a crisis was over she'd apologize, but wave off talking about it. Did he have the time as his career was taking off? When she was facing the frustrations of a beginning artist? She hadn't called his school friend, despite his urging. What was she going to be like when they were together in this small space? Would each rejection create days of gloom? A 400-pound black bear had lumbered into his cabin.

Enough. He jumped into his car, ignoring the driving rain, and headed out through tunnels of trees closing him into the night. His Chevy skidded onto a muddy shoulder outside of Holyoke. Water and mud saturated his clothes before he found some wood to stick under the tires. Ten miles down the road an all-night café lit up the sky, he stoked up on coffee, found Cousin Brucie's spot on the dial and cranked up the volume. As he drove into the city, sun lit the walls of concrete on his way to Maggie's apartment. On the fifth ring, he heard her padding toward the door. An uncertain smile peeked out from tousled hair.

"Hi, what are you doing here?" She reached up and put her arms sleepily around him.

"I can't stay long. There's something . . ." His throat felt like he was being strangled and he could hear each syllable croaking out of his mouth. "I have to tell you something."

She leaned back against the wall and rubbed her eyes. "What's the matter, Michael? You look awful."

"Maggie, I love you very much and I always will. But we can't get married. There's too much going on. I'm sorry, I'm very sorry."

She charged him, pounded on his chest. "You can't do this. It's not fair." He caught her fists and held her. "We talked about this, two artists working together. You promised. What happened?"

He stared past her, at the poster of St. Joan.

"Look at me. Look at me."

He walked over to the window, watched the neighbors going off to work. "I'm already behind on my book. If I don't publish it on schedule, I'll never get the money to make the payment on the cabin."

She slid down the wall. "We're going to have a baby."

He kneeled down beside her and took her face in his hands. Time passed before she opened her eyes. "Maggie honey, you told me you were taking care of everything."

"I found out just yesterday. I've been feeling really tired and nauseous. I went to that free clinic that opened up down the street."

He pulled her to him and held tight. "This is the worst possible time for both of us. Don't you see? My writing. You haven't sold anything. We don't have time or money for a baby."

"You got an advance on your book."

"It's not only that. We can't have a baby."

She shuddered and pulled away. Her face became splotchy, eyes wide with incomprehension. He sat beside her, awkwardly, waiting for her to say something. He waited. He'd start to speak. She'd bury herself even more tightly in the corner. Finally, at four o'clock he left. The next day he slipped an envelope under her door with the name of a doctor (paid for) and $500. Back in Vermont he called to ask how the procedure had gone.

"I don't want to talk to you," she mumbled into the phone and hung up.

He called again the next week.

"Maggie, how are you?"

"Go away."

He wrote a long letter to explain again why he had broken their engagement. Five drafts before he felt he had the right tone. He waited a week for an answer. Nothing. He called. She didn't pick up. Six months he wrote and called. With no reply, he abandoned hope she would forgive him.

* * *

Not a word for four years, until the reception at the Algonquin in New York. Now Michael was back in Vermont in the middle of the next book, Queen Anne, and the owners of the cabin had agreed to delay the final payment until it was published. His papers and books lay all over the large room in ordered piles.

A month after the reception, a letter from Maggie. She would arrive the next day for two weeks. Short notice for a two week stay, and two weeks was not what he had in mind when he casually dropped the invitation. But he had offered, and it was Maggie. That last day in her apartment, Maggie huddled in the corner. It came back to him, walking in the woods, in dreams, writing a scene involving children.

The cabin had a spare room she could use for painting and sleeping. He took the piles of newspapers and forgotten journals to the village dump, moved out a side table and broken chair, stripped the walls and washed the windows. Finished, he set the sponge and pail aside to look. With only a bed, dresser and chair, the room was large and light. This is what it might have been like if they'd stayed together.

The morning of her arrival dawned brightly, but by noon the sun was gone and clouds congregated. Mid-afternoon, the grey sky shuddered with sound. Rain pounded the ground. He heard a van pull up and went to the door. He could make out only that she was moving around in the front seat. When she got out, she spread her arms wide and faced the thunderhead. Nude. He grabbed a slicker from the peg and went out to cover her. She whirled. "Go away."

He retreated into the cabin, stood at the edge of the window and watched. He'd thought of her body often. Now, slick with rain and framed by the gray sky, the curves of her white breasts and buttocks shone, framed by green pines.

The storm moved on quickly. She grabbed canvases from her van, tubes of paint, brushes, and came in. "Where's my room?"

He handed her a towel and pointed. She went in and shut the door. Michael heard her setting up an easel, then nothing. An hour later he knocked.

"Tea?"

"Please, leave me alone."

He went back to his novel. Back to Henry I, ruler of France in the 11th Century, not an easy time to be a king. For most of his reign, Henry battled revolting vassals. His domestic life was no less troubled. After his first wife died, he married Anne of Kiev. Henry was not a particularly faithful husband. Anne was not a particularly faithful wife. She took a fancy to Count Raoul of Crépy-en-Valois and married him after Henry died. The Count's wife objected and appealed to the pope. He excommunicated the pair.

Maggie's door opened. She ran to him and gave him a big hug. He stepped back, a puzzled expression scrunching his nose.

"My painting's very physical." She paced as she talked. "My body absorbs the storm. I transfer it to canvas and need to do it right away. And thanks for the welcoming thunder."

"Glad to have you. Are you hungry? Pasta? Not as good as yours, I'm sure."

"Sounds perfect. I'll get the rest of my stuff from the van.

After the first forkfuls, he asked, "How did you start doing storms?"

"A few weeks after you walked out, I was on the Staten Island ferry and lightning hit."

Michael winced at mention of the breakup. She seemed blasé.

"I stood on the deck. The sky and water shone with slivers of light, arcing between clouds, crashing into the bay. The frenetic power of it went right through me. My hair was charged, electric, my skin tingled with each rain drop. I ran back to my apartment and put the sensation on canvas."

"I hear you've sold?"

"Your friend in the gallery on Madison came by one day and liked my work. So you know, I didn't tell him anything about us. I should thank you for leaving. I needed the space to get serious about my painting."

"So why come all the way up here?"

"You invited me, remember? Plus, I got a commission for the lobby of a new building in mid-town. A dozen large paintings, eight by eight."

"I'll be sure to order up another dozen storms in the next two weeks."

"Maybe more than a couple of weeks, but I'll stay out of your way."

He knew the two weeks mentioned in the letter should have been a warning. Maggie and time never had a relationship. "Uh, do you always stand out in the rain without clothes?"

Her face crinkled like he'd said something funny. "It's the way I feel the storm inside me. The total exposure gives me power."

The next morning, Michael was writing when she opened the door. "Will you show me the woods?"

They took a path through a grassy clearing flowered with pale red clovers and bright buttercups. At the end of the meadow they picked up a wide trail. As they strolled he told her about the more unusual looking plants, like the Jessamine vine with fragrant yellow flowers.

"What's this one? She reached for a plant with violet black shiny berries.

"Don't touch. It's nightshade. The berries are sweet, but quite poisonous."

She skittered back from it.

"A chemical in the berry affects the nervous system, pretty much shuts it down. Alexander the Great died eating them by mistake. Death comes with blurred vision, drowsiness, slurred speech, and hallucinations."

They rested on a swath of grass at the edge of a meadow.

"Maggie, you never answered when I called. What happened?"

"It was awful. The doctor did it wrong. The abortion was incomplete, he didn't remove all the tissue. I got home and I felt this weight in me and I was bleeding. I went to the bathroom and pushed and it splashed in the toilet."

Michael put his arms around her. "I am so, so sorry."

"A boy." Her face was a mask and voice monotone.

He wrapped her closer and pressed his lips to the side of her head.

"Michael, I came up here because of what we once

had. It was special and I haven't known it since. Maybe some of it's still there. I don't know." She shrugged.

"I'd like to try," he said.

They crossed the meadow, hand in hand, without saying anything more. Back in the trees, she reached for a plant with a three-leaved blossom. "What's this?"

"It's a trillium lily. The blooms are blood red or purple."

She looked at it more closely. "I want to take some back. This and some of the hemlock. Wonderful colors."

They were deep in the woods when rain began to drip through the leaves. He took off his jacket and offered it to her. "No thanks. This feels like a warm shower." She rubbed her hands over his face, washing it. Caught in the moment, they didn't notice the rain turn to pelting hail. Thunder cracked. A bright bolt split a tree twenty feet in front of them, the trunk thumped on the forest floor. The crowd of surrounding trees shuddered as if they'd witnessed a horrific accident.

"Leave me." Maggie took her blouse off. He didn't move. "Go."

He trudged back, frustrated by the way she dismissed him. He brewed himself a cup of tea to settle down and tried to work. Anne of Kiev also frustrated him. He hadn't been able to put blood in her veins. He couldn't get inside her head or capture her passion.

Maggie came in with lilies and hemlock branches in her arms. She laid them in the kitchen sink and went to her room. He heard scraping against canvas, followed by crashing smashing sounds. He opened the door and saw a new canvas quarter-covered, a brush through it, her body splattered with color, and paint tubes flying against the walls. A window was broken.

"This damn thing isn't working. I'm going out." She pulled on jeans and a top.

At sunset she hadn't returned. An hour went by, two. It was dark and cloudy, no moon. Michael worried. Black bears and bob cats roamed the woods. A couple had been attacked last year about five miles away.

He found her in front of the tree split apart that morning, head in hands. She looked abject and sorrowful. Her face was ashen, tear tracks to her chin. He picked her up, carried her back and laid her down on the bed.

"Stay with me tonight."

He undid the top button on his shirt.

"No, not that way, just hold me."

At daybreak, she rolled into him and unbuttoned his shirt. After that morning, concern about the length of her stay was forgotten. In New York, sex had been warm, slow and intimate. Now, depending on her mood, she rode on top and used her tongue, fingers, and breasts to keep his body dancing half the night, and showed him how he could do the same for her.

* * *

For breakfast, she gathered fruit and herbs for their muffins and omelets, claiming she had learned enough about plants and certainly was a better cook. Kept the cabin decorated with hemlock berries and lilies. Most days, they took a walk in the woods, amused by fierce miniature battles—a butterfly driving a bumblebee from the blue lupine, a bee defending his red columbine against a hummingbird. During the day, he wrote. She painted. When a storm hit, she went out, rushed back in, shut herself up in her room. In the morning, sometimes breakfast was ready, other times she was still painting. In the afternoon, she might finish early and lure him to the tree trunk bench set by the fireplace. They'd straddle the bench and be warmed by the flames and their hands. Sometimes she'd ask him what he thought of her most recent canvas. He didn't watch her storm from a distance, he was in it. She usually poo-pooed his praise, but continued to ask. Some nights, she didn't go to bed. He got some work done, but was falling behind.

* * *

In late August, a storm built up over the night, a squall line of thunderheads. Hail clattered on the roof, thunder deafened any sound in the cabin, lightning scorched the clearing. She came back after each cannonade, flung herself into her canvas, painted frenetically until the sky exploded again, raced outside, stood in the storm, came back, painted, went out. When it ended at dusk, she shut herself in.

Throughout this activity, he found a way to characterize Anne, wrote thirty pages, then exhausted, went to bed. In the morning, she was painting. He tried to write, but was distracted, wondering when she would emerge. The day passed that way. At dusk, he took a walk. The woods were alive with creatures whose lives had been upturned by the storm — birds fluttering to find new nesting places, rabbits and moles scurrying for new burrows. He heard a rustle in the bushes behind him.

"You're writing about me. I'm Anne of Kiev."

"You read my story?"

"You used my body and my moods and even my puffy dark nipples." She stood two inches from his face. "I was just beginning to trust you again, silly me. I'm leaving in the morning." Turned and walked further into the woods.

"Oh, for Christ's sake. This is an early draft – lots of things happen between here and what gets published. Look, I'll take it out. Can we go back now?"

She continued to walk away from him.

He stumbled through the trees. Back at the cabin, he got in bed, tossed for hours, finally fell asleep. When he opened his eyes, dark clouds shrouded the dawn. He heard her moving around.

"Are you still thinking about leaving?"

"I fixed breakfast and laid a fire. I think it's going to be cool today. And brought in some fresh flowers."

He was hungry. The pancakes were good, his appetite helped by Maggie's cheerfulness. She didn't seem to be in a hurry to go and made him a second pot of coffee. Even so, exhaustion from their fight the previous night wouldn't let go.

"Before I leave. When we talked about our baby, you asked what it was like. Come over here by the fireplace. On the bench. Close. Like we do, you in front. Yes, like that."

She straddled the bench behind him. He waited for her usual embrace. Instead, a sheaf of papers landed in the fire.

"That's your manuscript," she said.

"What the fuck are you doing? All the work I've put into this book. You're crazy."

He stuck his hand into the fire to save as many pages as possible. But after a minute, intense pain traveled up his peripheral nerve to his spine, sped it to his brain to the cortex that senses physical pain. He screamed and gave up.

"Now you know what it's like," she said.

"Like?"

"The pain of losing something you truly care about.

Cold Beer

Last night Marlene walked into the cantina. Of course it wasn't her, couldn't of been, but looked a lot like her: blonde ponytail, crooked half smile.

Pedro's Cantina, a dive on the beach, sitting on stilts. It had a thatched roof, colored bead curtains, and a shorted-out neon sign that only managed the P and o.

Jack was sitting in a wobbly chair near the front door, hollow cheeked, slack blue eyes, hit-and-run blonde beard. He and one-eyed Enrique had been crowding the table with beer bottles and butts. Seeing this woman took Jack to a place he thought he'd escaped.

When he arrived in Cabo, Jack planned to stay a month. But he hung on and eventually cobbled together a shack at the edge of the barrio with rusted sheet metal, some tarred planks from the pier, and plastic sheeting. Enrique showed him where to find the stuff and helped lug it up the hill. The shack kept the rain out. Good. And the heat in. Bad. That was two years ago. He could go back if he wanted. Hard to get started though. He got up at noon. Down to the cantina for a drink and a bite, another drink. Certainly couldn't leave at three. Heat. But then you didn't want to start after six, the next town was a couple of hundred miles away and only desert in between.

Her image never changed. Marlene. They met because her son was in Jack's class. He taught fifth grade at Highland Elementary in Visalia. Thomas was a bright towhead, short and wiry, but a bit of a loner who got picked on. Jack watched over the boy during recess. Didn't stop every tussle, just the ones where Thomas faced off with more than one kid. Got to learn how to get tough, but you don't need to be maimed in the process.

Marlene didn't have time for the parent-teacher conferences: classes during the day, work at night. They did their conference on the phone. Brief, to the point: How's Thomas doing? What does he need to do to bring up his English grades? Okay, I'll see it gets done.

Last day of school, Thomas brought in a note from his mother. She wanted to show appreciation for taking care of her son. Didn't want to do it sooner, while her son was his student, but now. She'd like to meet him. Could he come over for dinner Sunday?

He put on slacks and a sports coat and drove out to a housing development just north of town. Sort of raw feel to it, sawn ends of lumber everywhere, newly set concrete and roof nails still shiny. Lawns coming in.

Thomas and his mother were at the door waiting for him. But he had met her: at the Spice 1 Club. The kittenish one called Nikki. He'd gone there for a bachelor party for one of his ski buddies. This evening, she wore a buttoned-up print blouse, tan chino skirt, ballet slippers, blonde hair pulled back, and a shy smile. He managed a pleased-to-meet-you-for-the-first-time smile. "Ms. Brown, I've enjoyed having Thomas as a student."

"Call me Marlene. He says without you he'd probably be three inches shorter."

"Reckon everybody needs a bit of taking care of some time in their life."

They went through the house which had been furnished by the same people Jack used, Ikea, but where his was raw and jangly, too-bright reds and blues, hers was matched browns and comfortable. In the back, a small patio, a postage stamp lawn, and beds of multi-color pansies closed in by a pine pole fence. Heat waves rising from the grill. Jack tossed a Frisbee with Thomas while she cooked. Steaks, baked potatoes, and salad, strawberries and ice cream for dessert.

She kept the conversation on him. Where he'd grown up: Santa Rosa, where he went to college: University of Nevada, Reno, how he ended up in Visalia: best job offer he'd gotten. He'd majored in math. Teaching paid off his student loans until he figured out something else.

"I like the people here, low key, friendly," he said. "And there's Bear Mountain and Tahoe for skiing."

"Skiing! I love to ski," Thomas cut in.

"You've been once," his mother reminded him, "and fell down ten times."

"Yeah, but I still liked it."

Jack thought about offering to take him. He liked the kid, Marlene was easy to be with and he wished he'd had some chances as a kid. He was eight when his folks broke up. Never did understand why his Dad didn't take him with him. It took a long time to abandon the dream that his Dad would pick him up on the weekend and they'd go out, just the two of them, his Dad teaching him to fish and shoot a .22.

Jack ended up resenting the hell out of both his parents for leaving and busting up his life. Raised by an aunt, in and out of trouble. It seemed early though to say anything to Thomas.

He asked Marlene about herself. All he got was that she'd moved from the L.A. area a couple of years ago. Visalia was a good place for kids and gave her the chance to study nursing at College of the Sequoias.

Thomas started yawning and his mother sent him off to bed. She wrapped him in her arms and embarrassed him with a big sloppy kiss. When he came over to Jack, they didn't know what to do and they ended up in a hug that was more angles than curves.

Next day Jack went for a hike in nearby Sequoia Park. Morning was foggy, no one around. He passed through the oak stands, trudging uphill along Ladybug Trail, mist hanging in the upper branches, Spanish moss grazing his face, Marlene's lips on his cheek when they'd said good-bye.

He got lost in his thoughts and what he knew about her. Until a week later. Ran into her at the hardware store. In cut-offs, dirty sneakers, and grease smudges on her face.

"Damn sink backed up and the landlord is out of town."

"Can I help?"

Back at her place Jack crawled under the sink to check the drain.

"Hey, move over. I want to see what you're doing. You might not be around the next time something goes."

A whiff of perfume invaded the small space as she wedged herself in beside him. He showed her the coupling nuts to loosen, then he scooted out.

Two minutes later. "Okay, new one's on, come back in for a check."

Jack squeezed in beside her, "Hey fellow, you're in my space."

He pretended a thorough inspection, tightening up nuts and testing the pipe.

They squirmed back out, stood up and looked at one another. He reached for her, but missed as she turned toward the refrigerator. She grabbed a couple of cold ones and led him out to the patio.

"Thomas is going to be sorry he missed you. He's off with the scout troop in the Sierras."

They sat sipping their beer, listening to the whirr of lawnmowers and the buzz of hedge clippers from the neighbors' yards.

"Nice being here."

Jack stared at the fence, thinking about her. His last relationship had ended a year ago, it took all of two months to go from inferno to ash.

"Good to have the company."

Marlene lay back on the chaise, legs stretched out, eyes closed. Every now and again she glanced over and her face wrinkled up.

"Hey, what's the matter?"

"Nothing." She turned away.

"You usually frown while you're drinking beer?"

She faced him, tears on her cheeks.

"I'd hoped to tell you, but I think you figured it out."

"Tell me what?"

"You were in the front row in a yellow Hawaiian shirt about a year ago."

Jack tried to appear clueless. Her eyes wouldn't let him. "Yeah, I saw you dance."

"That's not the kind of person I am." She straightened up in the chair. "But the money lets us live here. Thomas thinks I work night shift at the hospital."

He moved over and put his arm around her.

She'd been sixteen. Tale of the cheerleader and captain of the football team who split with his scholarship to Ohio State when she was three months pregnant.

"The easiest thing would have been an abortion. But I could feel him growing inside me. When his heart beat the first time I knew he was mine to take care of."

"I wasn't assuming anything, okay? The person I know is a great mom with dirt on her face."

Her parents threw her out of the house. She stayed with a friend who'd just had a baby. Both were waitresses, lookers, good tips, surviving. Then her friend found a topless place in Orange, Marlene followed, real money.

"My friend got into drugs, Thomas was about to go into kindergarten, so I moved up here to raise him."

Jack's miracle started that afternoon. That's how he thought about Marlene. A rough start though. A couple of weeks after they fixed the sink, a party at his buddy's house. People spread all over the small ranch and into the yard, beer floating in ice tubs, ribs in the Weber, guacamole dip and taco chips on every table. End of the night, Jack came back into the living room, he'd been out getting a beer, saw Pete, one of the guys who'd been at the Club had Marlene backed into a corner.

"I know you, you're Nikki, from up at the Spice 1 in Fresno."

"I'm with Jack now, back off."

"Not 'til I see what I was seeing up there."

Marlene blushed and turned away.

Jack grabbed Pete's shoulder, swung him around and slugged him. Pete's head bounced off the floor.

Jack pulled Marlene outside. "Sorry, that won't happen again."

"Honey, thank you for defending my honor, but you and me aren't going to work if you beat up on every guy who makes a smart remark. I can handle it. Promise."

They married at the end of August and he moved into her place. She quit the Club and went to school full time. Two years later, a degree and ER nurse at Tulare. Jack decided fifth grade was the sweet spot in education. The kids do what you tell them, plus they want to learn something. Went on to get a masters in curriculum and instruction at University of the Pacific, night school.

They tried to have children, but Marlene lost two early term.

"Jack, it's you I feel sorry for. I have my Thomas."

"No, we have Thomas. We have a family."

Ski trips and horseback riding punctuated their life. Didn't spend much time with other people. Jack taught both of them how to ski. Two years later, to his chagrin, Thomas asked, "Hey, you want to do that double black with Mom and me?"

"I'll wait down here to pick up the pieces."

And he taught them to ride. Same story. "Honey, Thomas and I think we can leap that creek. You game?" she said.

"I'll wade my horse through."

He watched with pride.

They took the occasional trip to Reno and Vegas.

"Can't go to school in Reno without knowing a little bit about the craps table." And Jack managed to win most of the time. Nothing big, usually a couple thou, once ten. "My understanding of probability." Or, according to Marlene, "Luck." Whatever.

The only fights were about Thomas: Her: "He needs to be studying more." Him: "Give the kid a break, it's Warriors/Spurs tonight."

The night Thomas graduated from high school, honors and a scholarship to Claremont, they picked him up from his graduation party and drove down to Vegas for their own celebration. See Garth Brooks. Then next day Jack won big, $45,000. They packed up and headed north. Talked about what they'd do with the cash. Jack and Thomas ran through a list of boats, ski gear, and electronics they would buy.

"Enough of that, you guys. What about a trip to Africa? Climb Kilimanjaro? You claim the Sierras are too tame. Nineteen thousand feet satisfy you?

"For starters."

"After Kilimanjaro, we'll ride with gazelle across the Serengeti on horseback."

Jack leaned over and kissed her left cheek. Thomas popped up from the back seat and kissed her right one.

Highway 99, ten miles south of Visalia, Marlene and Thomas slumped against their windows, dozed, Jack hummed *Over the Rainbow* and chewed gum to stay awake. A broadening glow of light lined the crest of the mountains to the east. The road was in the dark. Other side, coming toward him, he saw a big semi swerve. Shards of divider-concrete crashed against his windshield, the chrome grill descended on him, the wide eyes and wide toothless gape of the driver were in his face, truck lights drowned the inside of the car and Marlene screamed.

In the cantina, Jack sputtered awake, toppled on his chair, and rubbed his eyes. Enrique next to him. "That beer's getting warm, amigo."

The Second Coming

In Levelland, Texas, the evening of May 25, 1928, Jesus Christ did not rise at 7:20 as the Reverend had foretold. Ninety-eight people had assembled around Farmer Smith's cellar door waiting for a sign. Among the witnesses, Charity, the Smith's nineteen-year-old daughter, bedecked in a pale blue sun dress and flowing flaxen hair. She had a curious interest in revival preachers for a farmer's daughter. Sparked by a teller who worked beside her at the local bank, and loaned her a copy of *Elmer Gantry*.

The crowd heard the Reverend entreat God the Father to send his Son to them. The Reverend's white shoulder length hair fell, carefully combed, beneath a black top hat. A prophet's beard lay against his black serge frock coat. Charity was struck by the power of the Reverend's voice, strong enough to be heard to the far side of the cotton field. And by the poetry of his preaching.

Look down my soul on hell's domains,
A world of agony and pains.
What wretched ghosts are there below
Some once so great, did they know,
So gay, so sad, so rich, so poor
Scorned by those they scorned before.

Later, Charity learned that he borrowed the verse from an old-time preacher back east, Charles Spurgeon.

After an hour of oration and no Christ, the congregation drifted away, in singles, then couples, and families rode into the setting sun. Only the Graham Spinsters and Charity stayed to hear the Reverend's final plea, "Lord, our Savior, we implore thee, come to us poor sinners, come, that we may hear thy words, 'I am the resurrection and the life. He who believes in me will live.'"

When the elderly ladies eventually raised themselves, and brushed the dirt from their knees, he turned to Charity, "You should go into the house now, my child. I must see to the cellar."

Peering into the darkness, he whispered, "Sam, where the hell are you?"

Back in the corner, among some wooden kegs, he spied the splayed-out figure of the un-resurrected Christ. The white robe was dirty, his long blond hair disheveled, and the beard drifted off his chin. "Sam, what in God's name happened?"

"We was down here getting ready, me and Charity,

looking for somewheres I could sit until the time, when I spied these kegs."

"I smell liquor on you," the Reverend said. "This resurrection was going to carry us into Lubbock and every town in West Texas. Now we'll have to go five hundred miles before we find someone who hasn't heard of this debacle. Get up, you simpering fool."

"Think we could take some with us? It's powerful good."

The Reverend left Sam where he sprawled. "Christs are a dime a dozen."

Sam closed his eyes and started to snore. As the Reverend was leaving, Charity poked her head into the cellar. "Pa's upstairs wondering when he's gonna get paid."

The Reverend climbed up the cellar steps, took Charity by the arm, and led her toward the barn.

"Charity, a young woman like you in a small town like this doesn't make sense. I've thought about a new way to bring people to the Lord, and I can see you as part of the new path to Jesus, a big part. Come with me on a mission, heaven's mission."

"I don't know, go off with you? I'd have to talk to my folks some."

The Reverend looked back toward the faded white clapboard house and saw Mrs. Smith peeking from behind the lace curtains. He steered Charity to where the barn hid the couple, put his arm around her, and pulled her to him.

"Reverend Barnes, what are you doing?" She beat her fists against his shoulders, but he held tight.

"The love of God is flowing through me, sister, and directing me to show you the special love He has for you."

He was looking into cornflower blue eyes set among fair features. Thin lips poked out of his snowy beard and moved toward Charity's pink ones. He was close to pleasure, to the sweetness of her lips, to feeling the fullness of her body. Then, by a sharp stab between his legs. He fell, curled on the ground. Pain forced his eyes shut.

Time turned cottony, minutes fluffed into hours. Slowly, painfully, he uncoiled and looked up. Charity hadn't gone back to the house. She was there, looking down at him, the setting sun creating a halo around her hair.

"You could have made a small fortune out there tonight, Reverend, and personally, I'm into small fortunes. You talk good, real good, but you're sloppy. You have no organization. Depending on a half-witted sot for your miracle, really. If you're up to it, I have a proposition."

He struggled to get his feet under him.

"I'll go with you. We'll do the Lord's mission and all that stuff, but I'm calling the shots."

A mixture of hope and trepidation trickled through him.

"Number One. You need someone to organize for you, someone who gets things ready before you preach. That's me."

"Yes, Sister."

"Number two. We're going to Austin where real money is and you're getting rid of your pathetic costume and hair."

"Yes, Sister Charity."

"Number three. Touch me again, and you'd better hope the border is only an hour away, and you got yourself a fast horse."

"Yes, Sister Charity."

"Four. I'll take the fifty bucks you owe Pa, plus whatever else you got on you. I'm running the money."

The next morning, Charity met him at the side of the railroad track running into Lubbock. Today, she wore a strict blue dress, black Cuban heel shoes with ankle straps, her hair pulled tight against her head, and a tight smile on her lips. At 8 a.m., they flagged down the engineer on the West Texas-Lubbock spur line and in fifteen minutes were in the Lubbock station to catch the Santa Fe to Lampasas. Change there for Austin.

"Isn't this a swell way to travel," Charity said. "First train I've ever been on."

"I think I'd enjoy this trip a lot more if this stew they're serving us didn't taste like stringy jack rabbit," the Reverend said. "And there's nothing to look out on but fields of stubby cotton."

Seated side by side, the Reverend told Charity that he'd been in a seminary near Baltimore and left last year due to a misunderstanding with the rector over his ministrations to a sinful woman.

Charity found out later the truth of the 'misunderstanding.' Eighteen months ago, Barnes was expelled from St. Charles Seminary for transgressions that priests, even veterans of years in the confessional, were unwilling to describe in tones above a whisper. Born Patrick Francis O'Reilly, he had been the seminary's star—a booming baritone whose reverberations evoked God the Father on Mt Sinai and an unrivaled memory of New and Old Testament verses. The neighboring parishes clamored for the young seminarian to preach. One Saturday afternoon, Patrick left the seminary for a local parish to prepare for the Sunday service. Rather than going directly to St. Anne's, he claimed he took the wrong street car and ended up at Pimlico Race Track. He put the two dollars he had in his pocket on the 50 to 1 shot, Shooting Star, and won. He intended to slip the winnings into the poor box at St. Anne's, but a small celebration was certainly called for. He sidled into a bar to have a wee nip, as his sainted mother would have called it, and that's where he met Lola. As adroit as Patrick was standing in a pulpit, he was much less so sitting on a bar stool and Lola soon had the seminarian and his money in her room for the night. Patrick's subsequent appearance and sermon at St. Anne's Sunday Mass were sufficiently noteworthy to be reported in the Baltimore newspapers. Patrick didn't remember that day in church, even after reading about it. But he reckoned his future was elsewhere than Baltimore, so went down to Penn Station and walked onto the first train headed west. His cleric's collar was his fare. By the time he reached St. Louis, seminarian Patrick Francis O'Reilly had become the Reverend Jedidiah Elijah Barnes and the Second Coming tour had been born.

Even before she knew the whole truth, Charity didn't half believe him, judging mainly from the way the he stammered over his story about leaving a city for life in the sticks. Picking up that Sam character didn't seem fitting, either.

Charity left the compartment to freshen up and check out the other people riding on to Austin. When she returned, the Reverend asked, "Tell me, what do you know about organizing revivals? I am most curious."

She explained that she had attended three tent revivals in Lubbock to see how they worked. Sat in the last row where she could stand and watch. At the first one, the advance man sidled up to her. She pushed him away.

He said, "Just want to bring you closer to the Lord."

Her reply, "Hell you do, closer to you maybe."

"Sister, sister."

"But I have a proposition for you," she said. "Tell me all about this show, how it works, then maybe, maybe."

After he explained his role in the proceedings, the advance man leaned over to put his arm around Charity's shoulder. "I only said 'maybe' remember? Have a pleasant evening."

"Well, I guess you know your stuff then," the Reverend said.

"You just wait and see," she said.

The Reverend leaned back in his seat, looked at Charity for a spell. "It seems by now some boy would have caught your eye. You'd have had no trouble reeling him in, pretty as you are."

"Careful, Reverend. The reason there's no boy, there's no way in hell I'm going to end up with a man who only knows how to grow cows or cotton, that, and babies tugging at my skirts. Well, there were a couple of not-half-bad bankers at Lubbock National, but all-in-all they're a pretty sleazy lot."

At the train station in Austin, Charity hired a wagon and asked the driver to take them to the best hotel in town.

"Sister Charity, even with the help of the Lord we cannot afford to stay in a place like that."

"Reverend, the Lord tells me we must. It will give us dignity, and better than anyone, I know you do need that."

As they rode down Sixth Street, the driver pointed out the tall rounded towers and red conical roofs of the hotel. "Biggest building in Austin. Cost old man Driskill a fortune, all that brick and special cut limestone."

The wagon pulled up to the entrance, met by a doorman in a uniform with enough gold braid to shame a Bolivian admiral. They walked through a thick cavernous entryway into the main hall. Charity stopped stark still.

"Oh my dear Lord, I have never seen so much marble in my entire life. They must have taken down a whole mountain for this."

"Verily, this monument to mammon outshines anything I've seen to honor the Lord." The Reverend stretched his arms out in a hallway one hundred and fifty feet long with multicolored marble flooring and columns rising four stories to stained glass domed ceiling.

Charity sent the Reverend off to get a haircut, a shave, and a suit befitting a preacher and healer, not a circuit rider. She booked their rooms and went off to find a meeting hall. She decided they'd start with a couple hundred people, work up. She located a hall, then went down to the offices of the *Austin Evening Statesman* to place an ad, at their religious discount rate. Followed that up with a visit to the Zeta Beta house at the University of Texas, where she talked her way in, not hard, now in her sun dress, unbound hair and dancing eyes. The boys didn't have much trouble agreeing to hand out flyers for the Reverend's talk.

Charity sat in the lobby waiting for the Reverend to return. Some twenty minutes later, she noticed a tall man in a dark blue three button suit, vest, and a silver tie. Black hair, close on the sides, with a high part. Looked like the pictures she'd seen of Valentino. He came up to her. "Sister Charity, shall we dine at the hotel this evening."

"Damn, you make up good."

"Language, Sister," he laughed.

Friday night, at the meeting hall, folks crowded the meeting hall. The Austin High School band opened the evening with *The Old Rugged Cross*. Then the Reverend Jedidiah Elijah thundered God's word into the hearts of the heathens of Central Texas.

"Believe on the Lord Jesus Christ in your heart and confess him with your mouth and you will be saved. You believe, why don't you confess? The truth is you have a yellow streak. Own up, fathers and mothers, business-men and workers, own up and be saved."

At the end of the sermon, a young man threw a crutch in the air and ran to the front of the meeting hall, "I've been cured." No one recognized the lad, but were none-theless impressed. He was a Houston boy Charity found out at UT. The band played *Onward Christian Soldiers* at the end of the meeting.

"And now, before you go," the Reverend pleaded, "Won't you help us spread the word and work of God throughout his vineyards. Give, be generous when Sister Charity passes with the basket."

Back at the hotel, the Reverend said he wanted to sit a spell in the lobby. Charity saw he needed to bask in the warmth of his success. She was tuckered, all the arrang-ing, and went up to bed. Next morning, she knocked on his door to tell him they'd made $100. Knocked again, then slowly turned the door knob. The room was strewn with bottles and clothes. Sprawled across the bed and one another were the Reverend, a blonde, and a redhead, showing everything God had given them. Charity quietly closed the door, locked it, and hung the "Do Not Disturb" sign.

At four in the afternoon, the Reverend knocked on her door.

"How'd we do, Sister?

"Not bad for the first time. What were you doing this morning?"

"Comforting lost souls."

"Lost souls is not my impression of who they were, and I hope to hell no one else saw. You're going to end our salvation run quick if you can't keep your pants on."

* * *

Later in the week, Charity came back to the hotel before supper time. She'd arranged for the First United Methodist choir to sing on Friday and Saturday evening. Promised the pastor a share of the evenings' proceeds. As she walked through the lobby, she looked into The Club (the hotel's name for the room where guests brought their own spirits) and noticed the Reverend, two women and a bottle of champagne between them. The women, hardly more than girls, were dressed in the latest—cloche hats above faces with very red lipstick, bright pink and green dresses, and patterned stockings. Two minutes after the Reverend returned to his room, there was a knock on the door.

"And who's paying for the champagne for you and your lady friends?"

"Why Sister Charity, these young women promised they'd bring their many acquaintances to our next meetings."

"I'm sure they did. What else did they promise?"

"Now Sister, no need to be suspicious. I am trying mightily to bring more people to the Lord, and maintain a high tone."

"See you do. And remember our talk about discretion. Sometimes your activities are headlined, it seems."

"What do you mean?"

"Over at the University library they keep copies of old newspapers from all the major cities. I found a *Baltimore Sun* from last April. 'Priest and Prostitute Perform in Pulpit.' That's you, isn't it?"

"You saw that?" His hands flew to his face, only wide-opened eyes were visible.

* * *

After two weeks at the same meeting hall, Charity decided it was time to find a larger venue for their show. She rented out the Millett Opera House on East Ninth, middle of downtown. With two foot thick rough cut limestone walls, the House held 800 people. To ensure attendance at the meeting, Charity convinced both the First United and Bethany United Methodist church choirs to participate and use their pastors as warm up acts for the Reverend. And the UT Longhorn Band scheduled a march through the streets to lead people to the Opera House.

"You sure this will work, Sister Charity? What if only 200 people show up?"

"Dammit Reverend, they'll be there. You do your part."

"Sister, what have I told you about language?"

The evening was a tremendous success. Officially, fifty people were cured. Unofficially, forty-five. Charity banked $400 in the Healing Lord account at Austin National. She was the sole signatory.

* * *

Early September, in the rectory of First United Methodist, Clyde Littlefield, coach of the UT football team and church elder, was visiting the pastor when Charity and the Reverend called.

"Heard about your work, Reverend. Always pleased to make the acquaintance of people toiling in the Lord's vineyard," Coach said.

"It's just so difficult to reach out to everyone," the Reverend said.

The four nodded in agreement, then were quiet for a spell. Looked at one another.

"What if...?"

"Do you think...?"

"I got it," Charity said. "Coach, your first game is against St. Edwards. No way UT can't win, is there?"

"If we don't, I better find me a new job."

"What say, right after the game is over, the band comes on the field, plays *Since Jesus Came into My Heart*, a real rouser, then the Reverend here gives one of his up-lifting sermons, a few more hymns, we do a giving?"

"That's a real ballsy idea, young lady. Pardon me ma'am. Reverend, you got yourself a great thinker here. Glad she's working for the Lord. I have to talk to the President of the University, but I think you can consider it a done deal."

On Saturday, forty thousand people filled Texas Memorial Stadium. UT won, 32-0. On Monday, the Healing Lord account at Austin National Bank won by $2500. On her way back from the bank, passing by The Club, Charity saw the Reverend holding court for seven young ladies, all very apparently fueled on champagne. She had the maid open his room and waited. An hour later, he stumbled through the door with two of the women. Seeing Charity, he pulled himself erect and sober. The ladies did a quick turnaround.

"Why Sister Charity, what brings you to my rooms?"

"Reverend, it is time to go our separate ways."

She sat calmly back in the wing chair.

"But who will organize my meetings?"

"I found me a man, a lawyer. We're moving to Dallas."

He twisted his long face in a way she found most unattractive. "What about the money I made?"

"We made. You'll get your share, less expenses. Remember, champagne is not cheap."

He started to pace back and forth.

"If I do not receive my fair portion, my lawyer friends will be called in."

"Reverend, you certainly recall first Corinthians 13:13?"

"And now abideth Faith, Hope, and Charity, and of these, the greatest is Charity?"

"That's the one. And charitably, I won't say a word about what I read in the eastern papers."

A year or so later, Charity picked up the *Dallas Morning News* and found a small article on page five. The Reverend Jedidiah Elijah Barnes held a revival meeting for forty-three people in the town of Dripping Springs. The article said he promised believers the second coming of Jesus.

A Little Love, A Little Shove

For Margaret, the anniversary night ended in the emergency room at St. Mary's Hospital with a swollen eye, a gash on her cheek, and bruises on her arms. For Rafe, the next day he was slapped with a restraining order against seeing her. Four months later he raped her.

The night had started as a celebration of one year living together. His high school friends had given them two months, tops. For starters, Margaret was Chinese, short, flat chested, small almond eyes flush to her face. She looked like she put on her clothes in the dark. Rafe was two years younger, Mayan, lanky, high cheek bones, black wavy hair, and dressed in polo shirts and chinos, not the ringer Ts and saggy jeans other guys wore. They said, for him, it had to be the sex.

Now she was in the District Attorney's office. The DA reminded her of Grandfather who took care of her when she was little. They were both big men in rumpled clothes, quick little smiles, and faces that wrinkled up when they listened. Like her grandfather, the DA had papers and books scattered all over his desk.

"People say I'm to blame, but that's not how it was."

Jim Leary leaned across the desk.

"Margaret, don't be down on yourself. Even though you were going together, the jury will hear that Rafe has a history of violence. He's been reported to the police twice now."

She noticed his soft eyes. Like her grandfather's. Leary explained that Rafe's attorney would base the defense on her relationship with Rafe.

"Remember to stay calm. Don't let him rattle you. Take your time answering."

She squeezed her eyes against the memories of the night of the beating and the night of the rape, but couldn't remember whether it was the pink sweater or the red one that got ripped, or where the shoes she wore to the beach were. She could remember the coppery smell of her blood and the pain inside the doctors couldn't heal. Leary came around from behind his desk and sat in the chair beside her.

"He'll bore in on the fact that you willingly saw Rafe after the temporary restraining order was issued. You have to tell the truth about this."

"That's the way it was with Rafe. He'd get mad, but I could calm him down. And he'd be nice after. Now I don't know." She wrapped her arms around her stomach. "He hurt me so bad."

When she got up to go, the DA took her hand. She felt she had put on a mitten, warm and safe.

"Let's hope your testimony will convince the jury of his guilt. This office will do everything possible to see that he is convicted."

* * *

The courtroom was large and high, a room originally designed for an era of dark wooden paneling, heavy velvet curtains, and imposing chandeliers. In the fifties, it had been stripped to a sterile room with white walls, chenille drapes, and blond furniture with sharp edges. Margaret looked at Rafe and his lawyer at the defense table, heads nodding. Last night she dreamed she was shopping at Lucky's, pushing her grocery cart, her son in the baby seat kicking the milk carton, people crowding around her, How can you accuse him? The two of you were doing it. Being trapped in the in the frozen food aisle, customers wearing masks, the faces of classmates. They tugged at her hair, poked her arms with their fingers, put their faces in hers, laughed and laughed.

The air conditioning in the courtroom blew straight down onto her legs. Usually she wore slacks, but Leary told her to wear a skirt for court. She found a gray one her mother had worn to an aunt's funeral. Big around the waist. The front pleat kept shifting to the side as she walked and she had to tug it back into place.

"You look nice," Leary said when he saw her.

From the witness box, Margaret glanced over to see what kind of people were on the jury, two women and most of the men were young. Leary had said he would try to get at least six women. *They'll be your allies here.* She'd never thought of women as allies. Teachers looked right through her. When she walked into class, the other girls rolled their eyes and only half whispered, *Where'd she get that blouse?*

Leary led her gently through the details of the beating and rape during the Tuesday morning session. Rafe's lawyer began the cross examination after the lunch break. Joseph Carbone walked slowly toward the front of the courtroom. He wore a dark blue suit, silk tie, and combed back silver hair. Rafe's father must be paying him a lot. As he reached the witness box, he smiled and said he needed to ask a couple of questions about what happened at the motel. She was expecting a growl, but his voice purred. Maybe he wasn't going to be so scary.

"Ms. Liu, you testified previously that Rafael Quintal beat you in a motel room last June." Carbone looked toward her, then to the jury. "Can you tell the members of the jury what happened that evening?" He waited, played with one of his cuff links, then looked away.

She dug her nails into her palms. "We were in bed, having sex and in the middle of it he hit me in the head and punched me."

She closed her eyes. Rafe had suggested they go to a nice place to celebrate their year together. *We'll light the room with candles.* Sometimes, he was kind of romantic. When they first met, he'd bring her flowers and candy. She'd felt special. But this motel room near the ocean had ugly green walls, a stained shag rug, and a damp salty smell.

"Did you hit him?"

"I don't think so."

"I don't think so?" Carbone paused and faced the jury. "But it is possible you could have hit him first?"

He asked the next question so quickly she didn't have a chance to answer. "While this was happening, did Mr. Quintal say anything?"

"He kept screaming. He was going, *Why did you yell 'Jason'?* I don't remember saying that."

"Who is Jason?"

Carbone's voice was smooth and soft, but his small black eyes made her panicky. She looked down. She was afraid he would discover something. Like Jason was a guy she'd been with. If Rafe had known, he'd of blown. One time when he got mad, he clipped her hard on the side of the neck. It hurt for a week. She stared at the back of the courtroom, thought about how often she'd seen her father smack her mother. The only time her mother didn't have bruises was during New Year celebrations when families got together. She asked her mother about it. *It's something men do when they get mad. That's the way it was with my parents back in Guangzhou. I remember my mother being thrown against the wall when all she did was say good morning to a neighbor man.* Rafe hadn't been that bad, not until that night.

"I know it made Rafe mad when I said Jason's name, but that's no reason for him to hurt me like he did."

"If I understand correctly then, Ms. Liu, you've also had sex with this Jason? While you were living with Mr. Quintal?"

She nodded. Carbone didn't make her say it out loud for the court reporter.

"Ms. Liu, I feel I have to ask, were there others besides Jason?"

"Objection, your honor." Leary rose from his chair.

"Question withdrawn," Carbone whispered.

Carbone paused and looked down at his notes. "And who bought the vodka you drank that night, Ms. Liu? Neither you nor Mr. Quintal were twenty-one at the time."

Margaret's lips trembled, her breath became shallow. "I did."

"You are two years older than Mr. Quintal. In addition, you are a single mother."

Rafe made her feel like a girl, not a mother.

* * *

For a year, Margaret and Rafe passed in the hall at George Washington High. He'd be in the middle of a bunch of guys and girls, joking and laughing, but always slowed down to give her a look. After school one day, he was outside leaning against the fence when she came out. "Hey, a bunch of us are going clubbing Saturday, I was wondering if you'd like to go?"

Rafe was smooth. When he picked her up, he presented her with a single pink rose. He paid for everything and he introduced her to people at the clubs. He held doors for her. Within the month, he'd told her about a secluded spot he'd found in Golden Gate Park. She could tell by the way he fumbled with the rubber that this was his first time. His charm offensive didn't taper off, even after the sex. He'd surprise her with a silver bracelet or a truffle from Schmitt's.

They'd been going out for six months when he began to spend most days and nights with Margaret in her parents' apartment. For him, an escape from living with his mother. His parents divorced two years earlier. Her accusations (some true, most false) of the father's affairs drove him out of the house. According to Rafe, her screaming and yelling had been going on so long, she didn't know how to stop. *If I was late or something "Just like your father, an unfaithful no-account."*

When Rafe stayed, Mable wrote some of his history papers. Little things like that. Made sure he was happy in bed. He learned quickly. She liked the weight of him on top. Quick, athletic, not a sack of sand like some of the others. And, he held her close, cuddled afterward, whispered words in Spanish she didn't understand, but they sounded tender.

In the apartment, her two-year-old son, Lowell, had a separate room, closer in size to a closet. He was the result of her freshman year hook up with a twenty-year-old guy she'd met at Ocean Beach around a bonfire. But he left town after she told him she was going to have the baby. Margaret had thought this guy would take her away from her parents' yelling and fighting.

Rafe played with Lowell, tossed him in the air, rolled on the floor with him and taught him baby karate chops. She dreamt about living in their own apartment, a nice one, Rafe's father, in real estate, would help the three of them, someday soon. Then her parents wouldn't be ashamed of her and remind her every time they went to a family wedding she needed to find a husband.

* * *

That night in the motel, when Margaret managed to wrench free of Rafe, she locked herself in the bathroom. She came out and dressed, hoping he'd calmed down, but he started up yelling and throwing bottles. She ran from the room, grabbed a cab, and called the police. They took her to the emergency room. At the hospital, she couldn't believe the face she saw in the mirror was hers. Raw, red, and pulpy. Like her mother's when Margaret was eight. Her father came home at two in the morning, drunk and yelling so loud he woke her up. Her mother tried to shush him, but he got louder. Margaret peeked out of her bedroom to see her mother, hands on her face, shoved against the coffee table, on the floor, her father kicking her in the stomach.

After the fight at the motel, Margaret didn't want to press charges against Rafe or get a restraining order. She'd be more careful about what she said the next time. But the cop scared her. *Look, without a temporary restraining order he's going to come around crying, saying he's sorry, but that don't mean shit. The next time, you could end up dead.*

When she came home her parents were waiting in the living room. Her mother shrieked, *How much more shame can you bring on this family?* slapped her, and would have continued but her father grabbed her and threw her on the sofa. *Hasn't she been through enough?* He put his arm around Margaret and led her to her room. *Your mother doesn't understand things.*

* * *

Carbone stood between the witness box and the jury.

"Ms. Liu, after the restraining order was issued, did you call Mr. Quintal and ask to see him?"

She glanced over and saw the juror with buzz-cut blond hair roll his eyes. *He's thinking I'm stupid and cheap.* If she admitted she called, they'd never believe she wasn't asking for it. She hadn't wanted to lose him. She liked living with him. When they walked anywhere she put her hands around his bicep. She could tell he liked it there by the way he flexed his muscles. They had good times, laughed about Bart Simpson's pranks.

"I don't remember." She looked at Leary. He pursed his lips, but nodded gently.

Carbone walked slowly back to the defense table and paged through a thick transcript. "Your honor, I would like to read from Ms. Liu's deposition. The question was, 'Did you call Mr. Quintal after the TRO against him was issued?' Her answer was, 'Yes, I did.'" Carbone looked at the jury, raised his shoulders and spread his hands, palms up.

Margaret wished there were a place to hide. The two women jurors looked puzzled. The chubby one with short mousy hair and a gold cross around her neck shook her head.

* * *

Margaret had phoned Rafe a week after the temporary restraining order was issued. Convinced him he wouldn't get into trouble since she made the call. She had reason to want him close by.

Two weeks before their fight in the motel, she'd seen Rafe and Patty sitting in the library during a break. Patty was a dark-eyed blonde in a tight yellow spandex top. Heads together, they were talking, laughing, eyes jetting back and forth to see if anyone was around. When Rafe got up to go, Patty put her hand on his arm and flashed a wide smile, "See you soon, Rafael," dragging out his name's full three-syllable Spanish pronunciation.

Margaret saw a girl she could never be—wide eyes, pale skin, full red lips. A girl with nothing to worry about. A face that made her feel there was little hope.

* * *

Before resuming questioning after recess, Carbone reminded the jurors that Margaret was the one who initiated the contact after the TRO was issued.

"Miss Liu, you told us about what happened at the motel in June. Let's proceed to the evening of October 14. Tell the members of the jury what happened."

"Rafe called and said he and a couple of friends were going over to Fort Baker and did I want to go."

"After you stopped and bought the vodka bottle for these boys, what did you do?" With emphasis on boys.

"We went to the beach, drank some, and looked at the ocean."

After a couple of hours, they'd emptied the bottle and drove back into the city, dropped their friends off, and parked the car close to her apartment.

"He went on apologizing about the fight in the motel, how he really didn't mean to hurt me, but the idea of me with another guy made him lose it."

He kept coming on to her, kissing and wanting to get into the back seat. That dirty maroon Civic. It was Rafe's mother's, but he used it all the time, so it smelled like KFC wrappers.

"He was pushing me through the space between the seats to get me back there, being rough. I thought I could calm him down if I agreed."

"Was that the reason you agreed?" Carbone stood beside her so she had to face the jury. "Or was it because you wanted to have sex with him?"

Not then, not like that. She couldn't tell what happened the way it was. How could she answer the question without it coming out wrong?

"He said he wanted to make it up to me for what he had done. He wanted to make me happy. He pushed my skirt up and pulled down my panties, and started… I said no, no."

"After he pushed up your skirt and pulled down your panties, you said no?" Carbone paused and walked back toward the defense table.

Her head felt like it was being squeezed. Her ears and teeth ached. Tears leaked from her eyes and nose. She covered her face but still saw that back seat. That night was a bad dream. Now she had to talk about it. It was real again. He shoved himself in her. The burning had taken days to go away. She wanted to forget, but needed to tell the jury it wasn't her fault. She wanted to pull her feet up and bunch her body so no one could see her.

She looked toward Rafe, still hiding his face from her, still doodling on the yellow pad of paper. Behind him were the two boys that had gone to Fort Baker with them, their heads together. She hadn't been able to make him see how much he meant to her. Maybe she shouldn't have let him drink so much. Even in the emergency room after the nurse yelled, Rape kit.

"He pulled down his pants and slammed it in me. I said, No! Don't! but he kept doing it."

"Are you positive you told him to stop? There are other incidents you've had trouble remembering."

"I stopped saying no because it wasn't doing any good. He just went on and on and something in me ripped. He really, really hurt me. I screamed. The next thing I remember, he was gone and policemen were around."

Margaret looked down and cried, quietly, streaking her cheeks. She looked up at Rafe. For the first time, he looked back.

* * *

Margaret was on the stand two days. The afternoon she finished, Leary took her aside and put his arm around her shoulder. "I know this was very hard for you. You did a wonderful job. You made a good impression on the jury."

"I didn't get to tell how it was, the way he asked the questions."

"Go home now, rest. I'll call you as soon as there is a decision."

A policeman approached them. "Mr. Leary, a quick question?"

While the two men talked about a scheduling issue, Margaret slipped out of the courtroom. She had to leave, get away from the courtroom, couldn't wait for the elevator, so walked down four flights of stairs, remembering the questions, what she said and what she wished she'd said. Her legs got heavier and heavier and she had trouble breathing. She sat down on the last step, out of breath. People stumbled over her. Her mouth tasted like last night's bok choy.

Five days later, Leary called. In the background, she could hear people and car horns. His voice was tired. The trial was over. Rafe was found guilty of second degree assault and battery for the beating in June. The jury voted seven to five against the rape charge.

"I'm sorry, Margaret. We did our best to convince them, but it's always hard when two people have been involved with one another. If there is anything we can do, referrals to counseling, things like that, please call me."

She played with her son until it was time for his nap, then went into her room, locked the door, climbed into bed, and pulled the covers over her head.

* * *

A week later Margaret saw one of the guys she and Rafe went to Fort Baker with.

"I guess you heard," he snarled, "Rafe got two years at San Q, thanks to you."

She felt bad, but didn't know what to do. She'd see her son practice the karate chops Rafe had taught him, so she couldn't forget the good times they had together. Still, it reminded her of the bruises he'd given her. Maybe when he got out he'd be different. They could start again. Other girls wouldn't be so attracted now. She missed his laugh and dumb jokes. She thought about going up to see him and asked her mother.

"Now I'm positive you have no sense. Hook up with a convict? Are you crazy?"

Her mother was right, but some weeks later she noticed one of Rafe's blue polo shirts that had been left in the back of her closet. Like the one he wore in the court room. She went on-line to check out the procedure for visiting a prisoner. Just to see how it was done. Write a letter to the prisoner to request a Visitor Questionnaire and mail the completed Questionnaire to the Visiting Sergeant. She didn't know how Rafe would react, but a week later an envelope with three pages of visiting forms arrived.

* * *

As she passed through security at the prison, red lights flashed and a buzzer went off. The guards pulled her off to the side.

"Ruth, take this girl in and search her."

A woman took her into a small room and waved a wand over her. It screeched under her breasts. "It's the underwire in your bra. Take it off and leave it, or go home."

Her head drooped. She unbuttoned her blouse, unfastened her bra, and put it in a paper bag.

The stale pea-green walls of the Visitors Room were peeling and littered with tattered warning signs:

NO TOUCHING, HANDS ON THE TABLE

Unshaven men in blue denim sat at big round tables. She didn't see Rafe, so sat down at an empty table in the corner. Each time the inside door clanged, she looked up. When he appeared, his face was thin and his pants were two sizes too big.

A mother and four kids, one in arms and the others under five, came in and sat with them. Their father strode out, a big black beefy man.

"Christ, couldn't you leave them at home?"

"Hush, they ain't old enough to know."

When the big man sat down he nodded to Rafe. "That her?"

Rafe mouthed a *yeah*.

Her words rushed out. "I never hated you, Rafe. That DA said I had to testify. He put it like I had no choice."

He reached out and took her hand. A guard's club smacked down on the table. "No comprenda Inglés, chico?"

They both jumped back. The big man shouted at the guard. The little kids bawled.

She looked around the room, all the men in too big or too small pants and shirts and the women and children in party clothes, sitting around on a Sunday afternoon.

At their table, the littlest girl had snot running out of her nose. Rafe asked about some of the people they'd hung with. "They promised me they would write me about what's happening and come up and visit, but nobody's come and no letters."

She told him her son remembered the karate chops.

She was now a teller at Wells Fargo and had her own apartment. Rafe got distracted by a noise across the room. She reached for his arm, caught the guard's eye and stopped. "You okay if I come up next week?"

Super Secrets

Susan stopped in the hallway outside her daughter's bedroom. Her son Thomas had just bounced into the room singing, "I've got a secret, I've got a secret," and closed the door.

Lisa was on her bed dressing her doll for a ballet performance.

A couple of minutes of muffled whispers, unusual for them, then Susan opened the door and looked down at her children. "What are you two doing?"

"Nothing, Mommy." Lisa had recently perfected the look of innocence.

Thomas blurted, "We're trading secrets."

"And who were you trading secrets about, young man?"

"Daddy and you and Missus Patterson"

In the small fraction of time her children hadn't yet learned to notice, Susan's expression froze. Then she knelt and gathered them in her arms, holding tight so her hands didn't tremble.

"Listen poppies, there's something you need to know about secrets. Sometimes you can tell somebody you have a secret and it's okay. But there are super secrets. With super secrets, you can't tell anybody you even have one. The secrets about mommies are super secrets."

"What about daddy secrets?" Lisa asked.

"It's different with daddies, they aren't super secrets."

"Thomas, tell me what you told Lisa."

Thomas cupped his hands around his mother's ear. "You and Missus Patterson this morning kissing on the bed."

"That's a super-secret. Do you understand?" She hoped she didn't sound too imploring. Her kids weren't completely clueless.

"I think so."

"Now off to your room for a minute. I want to talk to Lisa. When I'm finished, we'll have some cookies and milk. Okay?"

Thomas skipped off down the hall.

"Lisa darling, what's your secret about Daddy?"

"Last week, you know, during the party, I saw Daddy and Missus Patterson in the TV room. They were kissing an awful lot."

Susan gulped. "Mommy and Daddy like Missus Patterson a lot. That's why we kiss her."

"Mommy, are you alright? Your face looks sad."

"I'm okay, honey. Now get your brother. I'll be there in a minute."

Lisa ran off down the hall.

Susan slumped to the floor and moaned. Her lover's betrayal dizzied and humiliated her. She'd trusted Mimi. Why shouldn't she? Mimi was the first person with whom she'd actually enjoyed sex, who took her on a luxurious journey. She'd put her fingers and lips on Susan's body where no one had before. Now, could she even trust what she'd felt?

She went to the bathroom, saw the reflection of the deep lines around her mouth and her reddened eyes. The children can't see their mother like this. She sat on the toilet holding a cold wash cloth to her face. After two goes with the cloth and a bit of powder and lipstick, she was ready for the milk and cookies ritual.

* * *

A year earlier, Susan heard the slow rumble of a truck searching for an address on their tree shaded street in Roland Park in Baltimore. The neighborhood had been designed in the early 1900s by the Olmsted Brothers. They used the rolling terrain to create a pointillist play of light and shadow. Architects plopped in Tudor, Federalist, and Regency homes, whatever their patrons deemed impressive. Susan and her family lived in a gray stone colonial with Palladian windows set into a huge lawn. Pink azaleas clamored for attention.

A knock on the front door. The woman on the porch announced herself in hello-yellow shorts and blouse. Black shiny hair cut in a hard-edged frame around her face and wide red lips. In one hand, a pretty sack with a ribbon around it. In the other, the hand of a small boy.

"Hi there, I'm Mimi Patterson. This is Tyler Custis. Tyler's five, aren't you honey? I hope you like pecans, they're authentic Georgia."

"Happy to meet you. I'm Susan Symington. My two are at day camp. Come on in, have a seat out on the porch. I'll go get some refreshments. Coffee? And Tyler, juice, and maybe some cookies?"

"Thanks, we'd love a rest before we tackle the move-in. Ted, of course, is stuck at the office downtown working on a big tax case. Says it's worth a million dollars." Mimi turned to her son, "He'll just have to be happy with where we put things, won't he Tyler Custis?"

Susan watched Mimi from the back as she and her son went onto the porch. The new neighbor was tall and thin, with a runway walk.

"You won't believe how glad we are to have someone our age in the neighborhood," Susan said, coming in from the kitchen with a tray of cups and cookies. "We would have lived someplace else, but my aunt gave us this house as a wedding present."

"This is exactly what I was looking for," Mimi said. She had moved three times in seven years. This time it looked like they'd set down for a spell. Mimi was promised a traditional house in an established neighborhood. "Ted complained about the price, but I held that man to his word."

Mimi had been picked out of high school by a modeling agency, went to New York and had some spreads in *Cosmo, Elle,* and *Glamour.* Susan and Oliver grew up on the same street in Baltimore, were a couple in high school and college and married a week after graduation. When he was offered a job at Alex Brown, they came back.

"I'd better scoot now. Come on Tyler honey. Let's see what those movers are up to."

At the door, Mimi squeezed Susan's hands and leaned close, touching her head. "We're gonna be real good friends, you and me."

Susan blushed a little. She wasn't used to such sudden declarations of affection.

* * *

Three afternoons together and Mimi was telling Susan about the men she'd met while modeling. "Part of the business, casual, no ties, and if the guys, or gals, knew what they were doing, fun."

"Both men and women? And no one objected?"

"At the end of a day's shooting, whoever was willing

and available, attached or not. The shoots on St. Kitts and Bermuda attracted the best. A little foreign touch."

"And wives and husbands said nothing?"

"Hey, all part of the game."

"And no one got hurt?"

Mimi shrugged, "Not more than once."

If the weather was good, they spent their afternoons by Mimi's pool. If it was muggy or raining, on Susan's porch. One day Mimi walked in the back door and found Susan slumped over the kitchen table.

"What's wrong, honey?"

"Oliver came home drunk last night, lace panties spilling out of his pocket. I know he does it, but why does he have to flaunt it?"

"He's a bastard. You need a little TLC, the Mimi-kind. Come, let me put my arms around you."

Susan stood up and let herself be wrapped up in Mimi's long arms. The embrace made her dreamy. She was slow to understand Mimi's kisses. Forehead, cheek, moving to her lips. Susan pulled back.

"Relax, honey, it's all right."

Susan sighed and returned the kiss, until the side door banged.

"Mommy, Mommy." It was Thomas.

She clenched Mimi, then pushed herself away and sat down. "In here, darling."

That night she thought about Mimi. How quickly a comforting hug had turned into something else. She didn't know how to think about what she felt. She'd heard about this. There were a couple of girls in her sorority. Of course she knew about lesbians and gays, read about the Stonewall riots last year, but nothing close to home. It wasn't so much talked about among the people she and Oliver knew. What surprised her was how comfortable Mimi had felt against her. The warmth of her body, even through two blouses.

* * *

Mimi would go on for hours about her escapades in New York and on shoots, but didn't talk much about her husband. Susan had a hard time putting her together with an accountant.

"So, how'd you and Ted get together?"

"The short answer is long legs and a bun in the oven. Plus, he was steady and I needed steady for my boy."

"So, Tyler's not…"

"And I still do, but I get bored. Numbers, always numbers. He's a good man, but sometimes I'm so confused about who I am. Someday I'll tell you about me and my Uncle Roy, back in Georgia."

Susan reached across the table and took her hand, squeezed hard. "It'll work out, I'm sure it will, just give it some time."

* * *

"Sugar, I have a favor to ask." Mimi burst into Susan's kitchen. "Ted's boss says he needs to get into a club, for the connections. Everyone said we should apply to the Baltimore Country Club."

"Well, I'm not sure …"

Mimi shrunk back. "Oh, there I go again being gauche. I'm sorry, honey. What I meant is so we can get to know people around here. We want to settle down for a good spell."

"Don't worry, I know what you mean. We belong, and this year I'm on the membership committee."

"Why of course you belong, anybody lived here this long. So you'll put us up?"

Mimi took Susan's hand, kissed her palm, and skipped out the door.

* * *

Mimi kept prodding Susan to tell more about Oliver, but she wasn't used to doing that. In Baltimore, where everyone knew everyone else, confidences were not a good idea unless you wanted to hear from your mother or mother-in-law the next morning. Finally, toward the end of the summer she made a clumsy stumbling confession. The last time he touched her was before Thomas was born and then it was only his need for an heir. He claimed she was fat. She was a size 6, but his idea of perfection bordered on anorexia.

When Susan finished her story, Mimi threw her arms around her. "Why honey, you must be starved," and kissed her hard. When Susan went inside she looked in the mirror. She smiled at the smeared lipstick.

* * *

Now, in the same bedroom mirror: tears washed away memories. The children's revelations shattered them. No Oliver, if there ever was, and now no Mimi. Susan thought she was different from those slam-bang affaires Mimi had talked about.

* * *

A couple of days after Mimi's kiss, the Patterson and Symington children were at their last day camp of the summer. Susan's phone rang. It was Mimi. "Lunch?"

An hour before, she'd found herself thinking about

what she would wear. The morning was one of those hot sticky affairs only Baltimore can produce. An ash white sky and the sun a fuzzy yellow disc hovering close to the ground. The temperature and humidity, both 87. Clothes clung to the body the moment you walked out the door. She put on a flowery strapless sun dress and at the last minute dabbed perfume behind her ears. She needed perking up.

Mimi was in the yard as she crossed onto her patio. "Why, I do say, you're pretty as a sugar plum. Just look at you. But come on in, sugar's gonna melt out here."

Quiche Lorraine, salad, and a bottle of Sancerre were set out in a small nook off the living room. Space for only a pedestal table and two straight-back chairs. Susan's skin pricked in the intimacy of the space. She couldn't move without touching Mimi's knees. Their conversation was uncharacteristically disconnected, each saying something that did nothing more than furnish the silence. They finished the wine and sat looking at one another.

"Honey, let's go into the library, it's cool and comfortable in there. You set yourself down there on the sofa and I'll put myself here right beside you."

Susan didn't know how to start and the wine didn't help get her thoughts straight. "About last week by the pool."

"What is it, sugar?"

"If it was right or not."

"It's not like you're saving yourself for someone."

She was right, Susan thought. Mimi slid over, took Susan's face in her hands and kissed her lightly. "That wasn't bad, was it?"

"I don't know."

"There's no hurry, sugar." She laced her arms around Susan's neck and kissed her again, hungrily this time. Susan lay back against the cushions.

Mimi unlaced her arms and placed a palm lightly on Susan's chest. Her heart thumped. Mimi gradually inched the sun dress lower. "They're beautiful. Can I taste?"

* * *

Through the fall and winter, they were inseparable. Susan felt she had burst from a cocoon. Love was tender, long, and intense. Mimi had an imagination. When she was alone, Susan sometimes fantasized about a life with Mimi. Where they might live, what they might do.

* * *

Susan stayed in the bathroom a while to regain her composure. Now her children's voices became louder and louder, punctuating her mourning. On the way down-stairs, she brushed down her blouse and skirt, and strode into the kitchen. Thomas claimed it was his turn to use the red crayon, Lisa said it was hers for two more min-utes.

"That's enough, you two, put the crayons down, it's cookie time. What do you want, Thomas?"

"Brown milk and white cookies, please."

"Lisa?"

"Chocolate milk and chocolate cookies... Mommy, what we were talking about upstairs, it doesn't seem..."

Susan put herself between Thomas and Lisa.

"We'll talk later, the two of us girls, okay?"

* * *

Susan avoided Mimi for a week. One morning, after her husband drove off to work and the kids were picked up by the school bus, she headed next door and bumped into Mimi coming to see her. Her shoulders sagged and her face was blotched.

"What's the matter?"

"The Baltimore Country Club turned down our ap-plication. Ted and I so desperately wanted to be mem-bers there."

Susan put her arm around Mimi's shoulder. "Oh,

I'm so sorry. Lisa was home with a cough yesterday, so I couldn't make the meeting. These things are so unpredictable. But there are tons of good clubs in the area. We'll make this our project."

* * *

Three months later Thomas came running into the bedroom. Susan was looking in the closet at her summer things, deciding the flowery sun dress really didn't work anymore. "Mommy, Mommy, look, there's a big truck next door and they're putting all of the chairs and tables from Missus Patterson's and Tyler's house in it."

You Think You Are So Smart

The bullet struck my wife in the right eye. Walking down the courthouse steps with her boss, the DA. They'd sent Fat Richie Calabrino up for twenty-five to life, second degree murder. Cedar Junction State Prison was his next stop.

Jill's office called immediately. I raced home, found my five-year-old twins, Kara and Jason, with our nanny. They hadn't heard the news. I pulled Luisa aside, told her. She braced my shoulders, looked me in the eye. "Brad, be brave, they'll need you."

I put Kara and Jason on the sofa and sat between them. "Something very sad has happened. Mommy died this afternoon."

They stared at me, faces blank. "A very bad man shot our Mommy."

"Will she be alright?" Kara asked.

"No, she's going to heaven to see Jesus."

"When will she be back?"

"She won't be back, ever."

Their faces flushed, broke apart, and tears flowed, softly at first, then the three of us bawled.

Luisa came back in the living room and put her arms around the three of us. "I'll be here. I'll help your Daddy take care of you."

She made sandwiches for us, finally left around seven, off to care for her own kids.

A little later the twins began to nod off. I picked them up and took them into our bed. It had been ours, Jill's and mine. Not anymore. Kara and Jason finally slept. I didn't. Not that night, or the next week. Thinking of Jill, how I'd miss her, wondering how to manage two five-year-olds and my accounting practice, worried about how to get along without Jill's salary and pay the mortgage.

* * *

The police figured the gunman was seeking revenge for Fat Richie's conviction. A black Honda Civic Hatchback, sighted racing away from the courthouse, was found abandoned at the Back Bay T Station. A day later, the police picked up Vinny Calabrino, Fat Richie's cousin, driving the same kind of Honda. Blood traces from three different bodies in Vinny's car. Even without a gun, it was jail and no bail for Vinny. He was charged with first degree murder.

The *Boston Globe* headlined the story. A picture of Jill sprawled on the courthouse steps, fortunately her hair covered her face, next to a mug shot of Vinny, sullen and skinny. Vinny's lawyer claimed a frame up. Tried to make the police believe Vinny's car had broken down in Roxbury at two in the morning. And who's going to find a cab at that time of night in that neighborhood? So he stole the Honda from a used car lot and never checked the trunk. Plus, Vinny's wife said he was home streaming old Bond films the day of the murder.

* * *

Jill's family came out for the funeral. They're not my favorite people. Six years ago, at our wedding reception I overheard Jill's mother: Debutante, Harvard Law Review, and she's marrying an accountant? From Waynesboro?

We put the service off for two days to allow Jill's sister to attend. According to my mother-in-law, she was on vacation in Luxor, Egypt. "Staying at the Winter Palace, that's where Churchill stayed, you know. The Temple of Karnak, felucca trips, they're doing it all."

My in-laws are snobs, certainly, but they liked their grandkids and distracted them with gifts and trips. Jill showed bits of her parents' high falutin' attitude from time to time. We didn't have enough money for bleacher seats at Fenway, but for the Symphony, only orchestra would do.

* * *

At Forest Hills Cemetery, Mavis Anderssen, Jill's best friend, came up to me, took my hand in both of hers. In her lilting brogue (it was Mavis O'Brien Anderssen), "I'm sure you've been busy with Jill's family, but when they leave, if I can do anything. Dinner. Whatever." Then she knelt and smothered Jason and Kara in hugs and kisses. They'd spent a lot of time with her. Mavis lived across the street, two houses down, in a red brick Victorian like ours. She'd take over when Luisa had to leave before Jill or I came home. Loved kids, but couldn't have any of her own. Lost two, miscarriages. Then, she and Harold tried everything. Couldn't even get pregnant again. She wanted to adopt, but Harold wouldn't consider it.

Funny. Mavis'd always been cool to me. Didn't know why. Asked Jill, but she brushed it off. *Brad, you don't understand Mavis, she's moody sometimes, nothing personal. Other times she bubbles with joy.* One of Jill's things: me not being able to figure out people, numbers sure, but not people.

* * *

The police continued to work the Calabrino family angle, but the story moved from page one to a two-inch column on page 12. Vinny's admission of stealing a car, the dealer reporting it had gone missing, the blood not being recent, all this convinced the police Vinny wasn't the killer. Vinny helped his case by paying the car dealer twice the sticker price.

The last story in the *Globe*, some two weeks after the shooting, said that the VIN, chassis and engine numbers had been removed from the car abandoned by the Back Bay T station. Probably bought on Craig's list. No way to trace it to the last owner.

Vinny was released. The cops had three new cases to investigate.

* * *

I went back to work and the kids back to school. I had a new practice specializing in tax returns for small businesses. My biggest client had pulled a fast one, expensed his wife's Ferrari as two delivery trucks and wanted me to slip it past the IRS. I told him I wouldn't. The loss of his fees and Jill's salary will make it tough sledding.

A week later, the kids had half a day and Luisa had a dental appointment. I called Mavis, hoping she'd be able to help out. "When do you want me there? What would you like for dinner?"

I walked in at six to see Mavis, Kara, and Jason running around the living room playing Duck, Duck, Goose, banging into tables and lamps. Seemed she knew what to do with kids. A kid herself around Kara and Jason. Short, wiry and limber. Yoga and weights, she said. Dinner was perfect: barbeque beef and biscuit dish, first good meal we'd had in a long while.

In those first days, when Kara and Jason began to cry, Mavis would hold them in her arms, then they'd act out "Hug of War" from *Where the Sidewalk Ends*.

Mavis started, "Kara, you hug, Jason, you giggle."

Kara chimed in, "And we all roll on the rug."

Jason's cue, "Now everyone kisses, everyone grins, everyone cuddles, everyone wins."

The finale: Mavis sandwiched by the twins, long red hair between two curly blondes. Sometimes I saw Jill. Memory playing tricks. But Jill, ever the adult, even when she played, taught the kids words, numbers, animal names.

Harold didn't seem to mind the time Mavis spent with us. He was a project engineer for Oracle with a schedule to cry for—Sunday night, fly to Cleveland, work, fly to Bangor, work, fly to Asheville, work, fly home. He and Mavis met in London. He was managing an engagement at Barclays Bank. She was studying art and design at Central St. Martin's College. Originally from Belfast, daughter of a policeman, oldest in a family of five girls. After the mother died, Mavis took over.

Harold came across as someone used to getting his own way. Son of a Norwegian ship captain, carried authority naturally. He was some ten years older, a foot taller, and probably a hundred pounds heavier than his wife. But Mavis had her own way of handling him. She told me, "Cuddle him when he's close, ignore him when he's away."

* * *

Word of my limited cooking repertoire leaked out, the kids no doubt. One night a casserole dish with chicken cacciatore appeared on the kitchen counter. Called Mavis to thank her and asked for the recipe. She suggested a private class.

A few nights later she brought over little white hats for me and the kids and a chef's toque for herself. Jason was assigned pepper and tomato chopping, Kara, mushrooms and onions, me, the chicken.

"Jason, peppers need to be cut in twenty pieces, not two."

"Kara, onions are always tough, let me wipe your eyes."

The twins set the kitchen table, but Mavis moved us into the dining room. First time we'd eaten there since Jill's death. They were quiet, looked down at their plates, poked at the chicken and answered our questions with "yups" and "nopes." They got weepy so we picked them up, carried them into the living room and held on a while.

The week before Thanksgiving, Mavis came over, taught me how to make beef stew. A storm raged. Lights went out. We stood at the window to see if the whole neighborhood had been hit. Down the street, candles flickered in the dark. Our heads touched and for a moment the air was very still. She squeezed my hand and her lips brushed my cheek. In bed that night I fantasized about what it would be like with her. Not that I thought anything would come of it. She was a married woman; me, a sad widower with two kids.

Then a true nor'easter blew in, sleet streaming sideways shattering windows. Shut down New England. Harold couldn't book a flight back in time for Thanksgiving. Mavis fixed us a turkey dinner with all the trimmings. We were finishing up when Jason turned to Mavis.

"This is amazing, Mommy."

She blushed, I cleared my throat. Only Kara got something out. "She's not our Mommy, our Mommy's dead."

"I wish she was our Mommy." Jason's eyes began to puddle.

"I love being with you and Kara. You're the most won-derfulest bravest children in the world."

That got them back in the holiday mood.

The twins ran off to watch the *Finding Nemo* DVD. We stayed at the table. I poured some port. When we peeked in on them, they'd fallen asleep. We carried them to their room and tucked them in.

I could blame the port, or the weather, or missing a woman. After the babies were born, Jill lost interest. Whatever, Mavis and I ended up in my room. When the door closed, she said, "Lie back, I will make you a night like no other night has been or will be."

She kept her promise in ways I'd never known before. Her hands, lips, tongue, and breasts touched me every-where. In the morning, we crept down the stairs. As I closed the front door, I heard small feet scampering on the steps.

* * *

The storm cleared and Harold came home. We didn't see much of Mavis. But one night she called to ask a favor. Said Harold received an email from his sister in Norway. His parents had been in a car accident and were in serious con-dition. They lived in Steinkjer, a small town north of Oslo. Mavis managed to book her husband on the last flight out.

Would I take him to the airport? Snow was falling and she didn't like to drive in bad weather. She'd watch the twins.

First time Harold and I had more than hi-and-bye minutes together. I tried not to think about "the night like no other," instead thanked him for his understanding about the time Mavis spent with the kids. He hinted it was taking some pressure off their childless situation, so didn't mind, even welcomed it.

Then he became a bit sentimental about his parents, how much they encouraged him, the money for his education, and regrets that he saw them only once or twice a year. At Logan, I left him at the curb. I remember how quiet the airport was that night.

When I got back, the twins were half asleep on the sofa. Mavis had her overcoat on, said the furnace was acting up.

"What took you so long, Daddy?" Kara asked.

"The snow was coming down harder and harder, I had to drive slowly to get home safely."

"A big kiss for your Daddy for being so brave," Mavis said.

At Christmas, Mavis and I worked overtime to keep the kids busy. A visit to Santa, Christmas at Old Sturbridge Village, shopping for presents. We thought we'd been successful keeping them distracted, but one afternoon we found Kara and Jason dressed in the clothes they wore to Jill's funeral, eyes closed, lying stiff on the living room floor.

"What are you doing?" Mavis asked.

"We are being dead, like Mommy," Kara said. "We are with her now."

I was spooked, Mavis jumped right in.

"Okay, Daddy and I will lie down beside you, we'll be with her too, and then bring you back with us."

* * *

One night, as we were getting in bed, Mavis told me, "My father's nickname for me was Queen Madb, after the legendary Irish warrior queen. The name means 'intoxicating.'"

She was. I woke up tipsy every morning from nights like no other. The kids became accustomed to seeing Mavis fix breakfast dressed in a robe, slippers, and morning hair. By Christmas morning they weren't too surprised when they came into my room and found us.

Jason chirped, "This is like it used to be, huh Daddy?"

Harold wasn't in the habit of calling Mavis when he traveled, but when he didn't call on Christmas, there was no explaining it. Christmas was a special occasion for them. Every year he created a traditional Norwegian tree, a Jul Tre, with ornaments and candles. She worried. Tried calling and emailing his parents and sister, but no replies. I suggested she call the Mayor's office, a small town, everyone knew everyone. "I don't want to sound panicked here," she said. "Maybe they went to a hospital in Oslo."

After New Year, Harold's boss called. A crisis with one of Oracle's major customers. Critical information was on Harold's laptop. The company sent someone from the London office to Steinkjer. Two days later, another call to Mavis: Harold's parents hadn't seen him and they hadn't been in an accident. Police in Boston and Oslo were notified. The beginning of a series of calls. Twice a week: *We haven't found him, no, no clues.* Then: *He never passed through immigration.* Once every two weeks: *No clues.*

Mavis and I talked about Harold. After all this time, she doubted he'd ever come back. Something fatal had happened to him, or he up and decided to act on his fantasy, a life in Bora Bora.

"You know, the upside to this, Brad, as much as I love Kara and Jason, I really want to have children of my own. I could adopt. Or..." She glanced sideways at me with half closed eyes, a look with which I had become very familiar.

Mavis had pretty much moved in and redecorated my place. Interior design was her profession. Jill had decorated in a style she jokingly called Arizona Eclectic: Navajo zigzag rugs, Apache reed baskets, and Hopi black and orange pottery. And the big tin mirror we'd bought in Guadalajara on our honeymoon. One day I came home and they were gone, replaced by original cubist paintings, abstract sculptures, and a silver white carpet.

"What happened?"

"I couldn't live with that clutter."

"But this? Why are you changing the twins' lives like this?"

"I'm sorry, Brad, it was just shouting bad taste. I want them to know what good taste looks like."

Winter's not high season for interior decorators. When I asked her how the business was going, her eyes narrowed and her freckles merged into one bright red splotch. "It's not! I'm taking care of three people, cooking dinner and running the house."

* * *

A heat wave hit Boston the first ten days of March. That's when Harold's body was found. Inside an abandoned dumpster, alley back of Centerfolds. Lying face down under a mound of trash. Body had begun to thaw and smell. Rats had begun to gnaw. Briefcase contained his laptop and thumbed copies of Hustler and Taboo. No passport or suitcase. He'd been hit on the head, then shot, according to the medical examiner.

Three days later, two men walked into my office and flashed their badges. "Mr. Leiter, we want to talk to you about the deaths of your wife and Harold Anderssen."

It was a scene out of a TV cop show. Suspect's line: *This isn't a good time. I have a client coming in.* Police line: *Here, or at the station.* I chose their place, a small room painted overcooked-asparagus green, four chairs, and a beaten up gray table.

"The bullets that killed your wife and Anderssen were fired from the same gun, a .45 with a silencer."

"What's the connection?"

"You and Mrs. Anderssen. The two of you spent afternoons together, even before your wife was murdered. And, after she died and Mr. Anderssen went on his trip. As a couple, your comings and goings have made for some interesting conversation in the neighborhood."

I knew where this was leading and tried to explain I usually got home before Jill and sometimes Mavis filled in for the baby sitter. After Harold went to Norway, Mavis came over every day to take care of the twins after school.

The cops didn't believe me. "Where were you when your wife was shot?"

"I'll never forget, at the office emailing Bill Riley at Bromfield Art Gallery about withholding tax. Ask him."

"We know you can pre-schedule emails, we want your computer."

"After Jill was killed, I took two weeks off to be with my son and daughter. Came back to the office and tried to clean up my in-box. I accidentally clicked on a link, supposedly an accounting software package, in reality a virus. Had to junk the computer."

Fortunately, I'd backed up my clients' tax returns on an external hard drive. The cops didn't like the coincidence, but all they had was their theory about Mavis and me and two bullets from the same gun.

"I'm sure it was a professional job, somebody from the Calabrino family," I said. "You'd have to be a pro to hit someone with a pistol from 100 yards away."

"You ever been to a shooting range, Mr. Leiter?"

"You know, Jill was only an Assistant DA, but she was the one that found Richie's bolt hole in South Boston from searching property records. She was really the one responsible for Calabrino going up."

One of the detectives yawned, wanted a coffee break. They took my order, left and locked me in the room. They switched gears when they came back. "And where we you when Harold Anderssen was killed?"

"I dropped him at the airport late one night before Christmas. Said he was off to see his parents. Last I saw of the poor man. Awful, finding his body the way they did. Ms. Anderssen still hasn't gotten over it."

I was trying to be very matter of fact with these guys. Rather than looking at them I focused on a faint stain on the wall behind them.

"Interesting, you're so well informed of the widow's feelings, but then if the neighbors are right..."

I noticed the stain looked like the painting Mavis had hung where the Navajo rug had been.

"One more question. Ms. Anderssen said her husband received an email from his sister saying that their parents suffered serious injuries in a car crash. His sister did not send that email and his parents weren't in an accident. You seem to know a little about computers. How can that happen?"

"Maybe his sister's email account was hacked. You wouldn't believe the number of emails I get from friends vacationing in London who lost their wallet and want me to wire them $1000."

"Any way you or Ms. Anderssen could have created a very similar looking account, similar enough to fool a reader upset about his parents' injuries?"

I looked at the spot on the wall again. It really did look like the painting Mavis hung in the hall. She claimed it was the artist's self-portrait. I'd had trouble buying that explanation, now I was justified. "How do you do that?" I asked.

"Well, FYI, anyone can get a yahoo.no account"

I was puzzled. "This theorizing about emails, have the police actually seen the email that Harold's sister sent?"

"No, we only have Ms. Anderssen's word that he received one."

"And that's all I have. So, if we are finished here, I have work to do at the office, tax season you know."

They came back to the office with me, searched it,

then we went back to my house (further delay and I really was busy). They made a thorough mess of it looking for any incriminating evidence. Pulled out drawers, opened cabinets, yanked cushions out of the chairs, tore apart the toy box. Found nothing, of course. Same result at Mavis's house a couple days later. Funny, I would have thought they would have searched both houses at the same time.

That was in March. In July, Mavis and I were sitting on the grass in Blackstone Square, near our houses. Kara and Jason were sailing boats in the pond around the fountain. Mavis hooked her arm in mine and pulled close. "A lot has happened and I know it seems soon, but for the twins ... "

That's how the idea of us getting married came up. Seemed natural: she loved the kids enormously, sometimes too much. She let them get away with eating only what they wanted and tossing their clothes around. But the most important reason, they loved her, snuggled into her, basked in her bubbling affection. Those were my reasons. Her, she'd be the mother of more than two children.

With what we'd been through we decided to create a ceremony for the four of us. A small colonial chapel in Newport. Mavis wore a cream-colored gown. Stunning with her long curls and tanned shoulders. Kara and Jason walked down the aisle with us and 'officially' were our witnesses. We timed the ceremony so the sun was setting when we spoke our vows.

The next week I arranged our finances. Hers were

a mess. I set up joint accounts covering everything we owned with powers-of-attorney and wills to provide for the twins. Had no idea Harold had been worth millions. Mavis said she hadn't either until the Oracle people told her about his stock options. When it came to the houses, she wanted to wait a while to sell hers. Had some decorating ideas to make it more attractive, so for a while we were a two-house family.

* * *

One Saturday, on the way to dance lessons, Kara asked, "Is Mommy our real mother? Was the lady who died like Luisa, just taking care of us?"

I turned toward her. I guess my face looked funny.

"What's the matter, Daddy?"

"Why do you think she's your real mother, honey?"

"Well, cuz that's what she told me and Jason."

I confronted Mavis.

"They <u>are</u> my children. Don't you remember the awful mustard yellow room at Mass General? You, beside me, squeezing my hand, pushing with me. You wore the old gray cardigan I never liked. Jason came out first. Once he made up his mind he just popped out. But little Kara wasn't ready to see the world. We waited forever. Afterwards, we lay on the bed, the four of us."

The look in her eyes, she believed this. I felt empty, an egg shell that had been sucked out. Had this happened before we married, I wouldn't have gone through with it. But a month after… Kids can only stand so much.

Toward the end of August, the headaches started. I felt lightheaded and couldn't sleep. I didn't argue when Mavis suggested she take Kara and Jason to her house for a while. She brought soup over every evening, I went to bed early, but nothing seemed to work. Made an appointment with the doctor. He poked and prodded, took blood and urine samples.

"Doc, I know you've got to be tired of people diagnosing themselves with WebMD and the net, but my symptoms seem to line up with arsenic poisoning."

"I really doubt it, I'll order the tests run for it if you want," he said. "By the way, you been remodeling? Sometimes there is lead paint in old houses. Could be the cause of the fatigue. And check the plumbing, old pipes will do it, too."

Made sense, our house is 100 years old, but we hadn't been remodeling.

Tests came back. I was right. Normal arsenic level in the blood is 50. Mine was 400. The doctor wrote me out a prescription for Dimercaprol.

A couple of days later, I told Mavis I'd join them for dinner. The pills were working. I was thrilled to see the kids. "I'm better now so you can move back into our home."

"Aw Daddy," Mavis said, mimicking Kara's voice, "We all have our own rooms here, they're much, much bigger and everybody has a bathroom."

"Daddy, do we *have* to?" Jason asked.

I threw Mavis a glare. "Well, maybe you can stay a little longer."

Mavis cried, "Kiss sandwich."

September now, the kids back in school. I took off as early as I could that afternoon and went directly to Mavis's place. Knew she was at school picking up the twins. I'd have ten minutes to find the secret compartment she had shown the kids. In the dresser in her bedroom. "People used to keep their precious jewelry, gold, and silver coins there," she told them. She showed them her grandmother's shiny silver and sapphire bracelet.

The dresser was a Colonial ball and claw style, eight drawers and a tall mirror. Raised about a foot off the floor on curved legs. Highly polished mahogany and brass handles. I started with the top drawers, carefully removing bras and panties, one drawer for white ones, one for black and one for red. I searched for a false bottom, or false back. No hiding place. I replaced the lingerie carefully so there was no sign I'd been looking. This care ate up five minutes, but I'll admit that included time looking closely at lacy creations I hadn't seen before. In the next drawer, black and brown sweaters. Drawer below, blue and pink sweaters, but no secret compartments. I checked my watch. They'd be here soon. And on to the next drawers with red, green, and white sweaters. How many sweaters can one woman have? A car door slammed, the front door opened, Daddee! Daddee!

I hadn't found the compartment yet. This idea was not working. I yelled down. "I'm coming, I'm coming, up here in the bathroom."

I stepped back, looked at the dresser. The molding under the bottom drawer. Why hadn't I thought of it. Yes, a small button on the side, a hidden drawer slid out, big enough for a pistol, a silencer and a vial of arsenic. And now, they were there.

The twins ran up the stairs, "Daddy, look what Mommy got us. Brand new Nikes, Air Max 95s for me and Dart Vs for Kara. Look, shiny green and gold stripes, aren't they neat?"

"Now we can run fast." I grabbed their hands and headed out the door.

"Where's everyone going?" Mavis called, "Dinner's ready in ten minutes."

"Out for pizza, twins and me. Give you a ring when we get back."

Mavis was waiting for us on the sofa back at my house. Not happy, but managed to hide it from the kids. I scooted them up to their room, tucked them in, let them keep their new shoes on so they'd settle down and stay in bed.

Back downstairs, I went to the front window and saw two cars moving slowly down the street. Mavis came up behind me and hissed, "What kind of games are you playing with my children?"

I turned around and looked down at her. "I don't know what you're talking about, darling."

"The pizza run, what was that?"

"Bonding with the kids. Remember? I'm at the office all day."

"Without warning, when I've just spent an hour fixing your favorite barbeque beef and biscuits?"

I put my hands on her shoulders. "Some things are more important."

She pushed away. "For example?"

"Kara and Jason's safety."

"What in the hell are you talking about?"

I glanced toward the window, saw one of the cars stop in front of Mavis's house. A man stepped out of the car, climbed the three steps to the door, took a key from his pocket and went in.

"They shouldn't be in a house where guns are kept, even in a secret compartment, especially if their so-called mother shows them where it is."

"What are you talking about?"

"The dresser."

"There's only my grandmother's bracelet in the secret compartment." She scrunched her face in confusion.

I took a step back. "Well, last time I looked, about two hours ago, there was a gun."

Her eyes and mouth registered surprise, shock and

puzzlement, opening and closing randomly. She stepped back, breathed deeply, her eyes narrowed to pistol barrels and calmly said, "You are a dirty double crossing son of a bitch, and I promise, you will pay."

Red lights flooded our living room. The door burst open. The force of four burly cops knocked us back on to the sofa.

"Mavis O'Brien Anderssen, you are under arrest for the murders of Jill Leiter and Harold Anderssen. You have the right to remain silent…"

She sat there, gaping. Gave me the chance to ask, "Why did you do it? Why did you kill my wife and your husband?"

"I didn't kill anyone."

The police sergeant stepped in. "There was a gun, a silencer and a vial of arsenic in your dresser, Ms. Anderssen. And the gun matches the one used to kill Ms. Leiter and Mr. Anderssen."

"They're not mine."

Mavis slumped in the policeman's arms as he was trying to cuff her. Her face was twisted in disbelief. "Brad honey, how can you say these things? Don't you remember the plans we made for being a family, right here in this room, the life we'd have together, how you'd arrange everything?"

I turned to the cop closest to me. "If you believe that, you should hear her fantasy about giving birth to Kara and Jason."

"Okay lady, you're coming with us down to the station."

"But this was about our life, Brad." Mavis was full into her sobbing routine. "Our life with Kara and Jason."

"Then why did you try to poison me? Did you want the twins all to yourself."

"Poison you?"

I turned to the cops. "I have the doctor's records, and you have the vial of arsenic, right?"

Mavis broke from the cop's grip and jumped on me, pummeled my face and chest. I sat there and let her pound until one of the cops picked her up. Going out the front door he turned back, "I thought you said she was small." Her screams didn't stop until the cop car pulled away.

* * *

After the trial, I sold the houses in Boston and the three of us moved out to San Francisco. The whole affair has been tough on the twins. Bought a place in tony Pacific Heights and put them in Drew School. They seem to be pretty good, considering. I've gotten involved in some school committees. Surprising number of divorced mothers. I'm not doing anything special now, just taking care of Kara and Jason. They'll be seven next month.

Coming Home

Buda, 1839

"There are rebels in Borsod County. Where you grew up. They've stepped up their activity in the last three weeks, attacking then disappearing into the countryside. Take five hundred men. End this," General Bauer said. "And do it quickly. Vienna is watching."

Colonel Janós Hajdú stormed out of Cavalry Headquarters cursing. As he strode across the courtyard bounded by long pale yellow buildings, his mind filled up with bloody streams and trampled fields of wheat. He'd swum in those streams, cut hay in those fields. When he reached the street, he stopped, leaned against a pillar, covered his face with his hands. He didn't want anyone to see him trembling. But, as horrific as the situation might be, he couldn't imagine anyone else taking this mission. They wouldn't do it as carefully, or as well.

* * *

211

The officers' mess glimmered with candlelight and its reflections off the heavy gold braids of hussars' uniforms. The walls were draped with campaign flags and banners. A crowd gathered around Janós when he entered the room. Many of them owed their lives to his swift check of an unnoticed enemy sword or his ability to wheel a mounted detachment behind an attacking Turkish flank. He'd never lost a battle. He was proud, some of his superiors complained, to the point of arrogance.

Over port, he talked about the mission. "Gentlemen, this will not be easy. Our orders are to suppress a rebellion of Hungarian peasants. I am Hungarian. Many of you are, also."

He turned to the wall map of northern Hungary. He had ridden among the volcanic cliffs and caves dotting the Bükk Mountains, had smelled sulfur mingled with the anise of the beech tree forest. To the east and south of town were foothills. Beyond, wheat fields and villages.

"In small units, you will hide in the foothills and fields to capture rebels returning from their forays into Miskolc, pick them off, one and two at a time."

He hesitated. His senses racing ahead to the stickiness of August heat and stalk-eyed flies swarming over bodies in the fields. The ones his friends owned, the ones tilled by his tenants.

"Your job is to rip out the roots of the rebellion with a minimum loss of life."

* * *

Janós and five cartographers went ahead of the main body of soldiers. They arrived in the hills late in the day. The golden wheat plains below lay sprinkled with fiery reflections off thatched cottage roofs and threads of streams. He billeted the cartographers at the garrison and went on to his tenants' farmhouse. Katalin and Imre had worked for Janós's father. They were bent over their supper when Janós walked in. Imre wore his thick hair in two plaits that fell to his chest. Her hair was covered by a crisp white cap. A warm handshake from Imre, a hug from Katalin. She had a sixth sense about unexpected guests and his bowl was on the table in minutes. Her goulash could never have too much paprika and she confected her nokedli with air rather than eggs.

"You're early this year."

"I'm between assignments so I'll be here longer than usual. You'll have an extra hand for the harvest."

"The crop looks good," Imre said. "I hope this fighting doesn't get worse."

"I've heard stories. What's it about?" Janós asked.

"A collection of things. Last year the governor appropriated ten hectares from the village for his personal use. People got frustrated and felt they needed to do something."

Katalin cut in. "Tell him about Anna."

Anna, twenty years earlier, blond hair spread on the hay, her tongue teasing his.

"Her husband was killed by a soldier from the garrison in the spring."

"I lost track of her," Janós said. "She moved after I went off to the Academy."

"Over to Sajólád."

"Her children should be old enough to help on the farm?"

"Only a daughter, eighteen. Looks like her mother, but with her father's temper."

"Shortly after the murder, the rebels started their attacks. They're passionate about replacing the governor of Borsod, a stupid oaf from Salzburg."

"The rebels are becoming legends," said Katalin with pride. "They seem invincible. In the last four months, their worst injury was a broken arm."

"Anna must have relatives to help in the fields," Janós said.

"You should go see her."

"She probably wouldn't remember me."

"Her cottage is the small one at the west edge of the village," Imre volunteered. "There's a stream about fifty meters to the south of it."

"If I'm out in that direction."

"We're going to turn in now, see you in the morning," Katalin said.

Janós went off to the room he'd had as a boy, dreaming of galloping cavalry and clashing swords. The white washed walls covered with pictures of soldiers and horses. His father had brought them back. Otherwise, the room was simple with a bed and two wooden chests, one for clothes and the smaller one for books. The memories were comforting, but he couldn't sleep.

The news of Anna's husband resurrected feelings he'd tamped down long ago. When he was little, Anna lived nearby and they played on the floor of her parents' cottage or in the garden. They'd grown older and school and work in the fields took over, but whenever they'd passed in the lane a sideways glance of her grey eyes and a tilt of her head said *come along, let's play*. She and her family had been his refuge from an ex-drill sergeant father and a mother who lived in the shadows. Anna was, by turns, soft and warm, quick and fiery, and she could ride the wind. They chased one another on horseback across the plains, jumping streams and leaping fences. The day before Janós left for military academy, they swam in the river and lay in the sun, far from everyone. At sunset, they made love for the first time, urgently and desperately, promising eternal fidelity.

* * *

Anna sensed it that night, was sure three weeks later. She

was pregnant with Jan's child. And he had gone off to the Theresian Military Academy, south of Vienna. The next morning, she carted her peppers to the market in Miskolc, setting her stall in the usual place where the morning sun would warm those she'd cut open, creating an enticing scent for shoppers. As usual, István Kovács set his stall up next to hers. His family grew onions, parsnips, carrots, potatoes, and turnips. She teased him about looking like his produce, the long wiry frame of a carrot and a lumpy potato face creased by a corn ear grin. This week he brought her a huge bouquet of flowering cherry branches, sprinkling pink petals in her hair.

"So, is this the week you are going to accept my proposal?"

"Which one is that?" She turned shyly to the side.

He gave her a gentle poke on the arm. "Marriage, of course, you goose."

"You haven't given up, have you?"

"No, and I never will. I keep count. This is the fifty-sixth time I've asked."

"I guess someday I'll have to say yes, won't I?"

"Are you serious?"

"Yes, I will marry you."

He grabbed her around the waist and twirled her though the market. When they finally circled back to their stalls, their neighbors stood around clapping and laughing. He lifted Anna up on the table, took his guitar, went down on one knee, and sang.

My flower, my flower
Today you picked me
Eagles do not fly so high
As my heart when my flower is nigh

A month later they married and started life in a small cottage at the edge of the Kovács' family land. For his rambunctious ways, István was surprisingly tender in bed. He kept a candle lit so he could watch her face as his lips moved up and down her body. And she relished his care that she climax whenever they made love. Nothing like the stories Anna's friends and mother had told her about their men.

The joy István felt when Márta was born. He ran around to every cottage in the village, barged in, "It's a girl, Márta is a girl. She looks like Anna." But they were both scared. She was sickly. Would she make it? He stayed up with his daughter through the night, softly plucking his guitar until she slept. When she woke, bawling, Anna took her in her arms and he'd play another lullaby.

When Márta was four, he taught her simple cords. At six, she played entire songs. At ten, they were a duet at village fairs and weddings. "You see my daughter... how good she is. It's the Kovács gene. Goes back generations. Did you ever hear of my grandfather? He played at court in Vienna."

* * *

The news arrived four months after Janós left Anna for the Academy. It came through one of his father's former colleagues who taught at the school. Janós remembered the stomach cramps he suffered months afterward. Anna had married. Worse, her husband was a gad-about musician who grew turnips. He was shattered. He became prickly and fought with his fellow cadets. The commandant threatened to dismiss him from the Academy. His letters to her were returned unopened. On earlier visits to the village, he had ridden out toward her cottage a few times, but turned back. Imagining her with someone else was difficult. Seeing her would be impossibly wrenching. Her marriage was the reason he decided on a career in the cavalry. He had more control over what happened to him. Soldiers did things for reasons he understood.

* * *

Janós got up before Imre and Katalin the next morning and rode out to meet the cartographers in the foothills. He showed them what he wanted to have mapped—the tracks and paths the farmers and herdsmen used to cross the countryside, sure they were used by the rebels.

After the mapmakers rode off, he sat for a moment, looking over the tall grasses. He and Anna, when they were four or five and shorter than the grass, played hide-and-seek. She got lost trying to find a hiding place and he got lost looking for her. Her parents finally found them by following the zigzags trampled in the field.

He wheeled his horse, Zeno, towards the southeast and saw a track between two fields, about two kilometers long. He hadn't stretched his horse or himself since Buda. A chance. He sat forward and pressed Zeno's flanks. The gray horse exploded. He'd gone half the distance when he heard hoofs behind him and looked around. Another horse and rider overtook him, a dark chestnut stallion ridden by a girl with long blond hair. János spurred Zeno on, but couldn't catch the other rider until she was forced to slow by a muddy uphill track.

"Handsome Shagya you have. Not as fast as a pure Arabian," she said.

"Nice riding, the jump at the stream. Where did you learn?"

"My mother."

"My name is János Hajdú, I grew up around here."

"I'm Márta Kovács. Have to go now."

He watched as she galloped off, balanced and soft on the horse, then he continued up the rise. From the top, he saw the chalk-white walls and thatched roof of a cottage and a stream south of it. Anna came to the door as he rode in. The sun was behind him. She looked up, puzzled.

"Anna, it's Jan."

She took a step backward.

"Jan, Janós Hajdú."

He dismounted and walked towards her. She seemed trapped in a strange stillness, then turned into the cottage.

The contrast with his tenants' place upset him. Imre and Katalin had four rooms. Anna had one. The walls were bare except for some caraway, paprika, and bay drying above the fireplace. Wildflowers and books were on a table in the center of the room. Shiny copper cook pots beside the fireplace, next to them, an old guitar. Bedding stacked under a bench by the window. Four small food baskets in the corner.

She stood at the far side of the table and motioned for him to sit across from her. "Would you like some tea?"

"How are you? I hear you have a daughter."

"The harvest will be good this year. We'll be fine."

He looked at the woman who had been the girl he loved. The suns of summers in the fields left fine wrinkles framing her eyes and mouth. But there was the same light at the corner of her eyes and her lips were wide and full as before. And he could almost feel the tap of her tongue when they'd kissed.

"Tea would be nice. Thank you."

As she served, her hand accidentally brushed his. The touch startled both of them. They sat sipping, he made appreciative murmurs.

She closed her eyes and took a deep breath, looked up, about to say something. He opened his mouth and blurted, "I don't know how to start, for a long time I thought I'd done something or said something, I never heard from you, and three months after I left..."

She leaned across the table and put her finger on his lips. The touch was a surprise, but when he leaned forward, she drew back. Words stumbled out. "My father got sick, my brothers were small, and I couldn't take care of the farm alone. I had no choice."

"Why didn't you let me know? I could have come back."

Her shoulders slumped and she looked tired. "It's easy to say now, but your father would never have let you."

He looked down at his cup. It was true.

"I never told you about any of this. I knew you didn't like István and I didn't want to cause trouble. But, with Father sick and you gone..."

János looked away. "You didn't write."

"I thought I'd see you when you came home on leave. I wanted to tell you in person. Once or twice I saw you and I think you saw me, but you rode off in the other direction."

"You knew I'd be with Katalin and Imre."

"I couldn't. István was insanely jealous That's not the way he was at first though." He'd been silly, bringing her huge bouquets of wild flowers, dancing the czárdá, spinning and kicking around the market, a joke for every occasion.

"Didn't you get my letters?" he asked.

Anna blushed. "No."

István.

"I'm sorry, I should have written." She reached across the table and took his hand. "You must have been hurt never to have come to see me."

He bowed his head. "It wasn't an easy time."

They sat quietly with their tea, then to avoid the awkwardness of more silence he asked, "What happened to your husband, how did he...?"

Márta opened the cottage door. Grey-eyed, in a bloused white shirt and pants, tucked into soft black boots. Anna at eighteen, though leaner and taller.

Anna pulled her hands back into her lap. "I'd like you to meet my old friend János Hajdú. We grew up near one another. He's in the Cavalry now..."

"Oh, we've already met. We raced on that path between the Nagy's fields. I won. Doesn't say much for the Cavalry."

János laughed. "She is good. Said her mother taught her."

Anna blushed with pride and bowed her head.

Márta was the image of Anna he had carried from that last day they were together. He felt his face turn red. Márta turned to leave, but Anna took her arm. "Sit down. Pour us another cup and one for yourself."

She served the tea, but sat apart from them on the bench against the wall.

"I was about to tell Jan what happened to your father."

"I'll tell it. My father and his friends were in a bar in Miskolc. A bunch of Austrian soldiers called them Jews and Gypsies and knocked over their glasses. My father didn't put up with that sort of thing. One of the soldiers punched my father in the mouth and everyone started fighting. A minute later, one of the soldiers pulled out a gun and shot my father. It was murder."

János reached toward her. "I'll talk to the garrison commander."

She shrugged. "What's the use? It's over now. I don't want to have anything to do with soldiers," she said. "So why are you here?"

Two Annas in front of him, the desire for both of them to like him. "I'm back for the harvest."

"Why should we believe you? With the rebellion going on." Márta asked.

He flushed, unused to being questioned, "If there are problems in this part of the Empire, the Emperor would never send Hungarians to settle them, Poles or Croatians maybe."

"Márta, will you play something for Jan? She's very good, like her father."

"Mother," she sighed, "I told some friends I'd meet them."

Anna mouthed *Play*.

"Okay, a short piece."

She bent over her guitar, started with a series of sparkling two tone tremolos, followed by a melancholy fandango, and finished with a shrieking allegro.

Jan jumped up from his chair, "Brava, Brava. She's more than very good. Better than anything I've heard in Vienna or Paris."

"It's the story of our life, mother's and mine. Sweet, lively, some disappointments, then death," Márta said. She set her guitar in the corner. "I'll be late tonight, Mother."

A few minutes later, Anna walked outside with him. "Excuse her, Jan. She's bitter about what happened." She took his hand. "Will I see you again?"

He replied with a smile, mounted, then put Zeno at a walk. There was a time he hadn't wanted to see Anna. Now, he found her beautiful in a new way. A restive, suffused glow had replaced her shining exuberance.

At dinner with Katalin and Imre, János listened to the tale of their runaway cow.

"I can't imagine why she bolted," Katalin said.

"Can you pass the wine, please," János said.

His tenants looked at one another and mouthed, *his fifth.*

"Was that you this afternoon on the rise overlooking Anna's place?" Imre asked. "Looked like Zeno from a distance."

"I don't think so."

* * *

Janós and the cartographers rode out to check the maps they'd made. After an hour, they split up. Separately, he wanted to scout the routes from the mountains into the plains for the main body. First, he rode to Anna's cottage.

"I came by to see if you wanted to take a ride."

"I'd like that, like old times. Do you want me to pack some food?"

Janós pointed to his saddle bags. "I've got enough for the two of us."

"So you presumed?"

The tone of her quip was somewhere between coquetry and annoyance. He couldn't read her intentions the way he once had.

"I had hopes."

They rode through old beech forests and grassy meadows of violet-blue gentian and yellow yarrow. A saker falcon, gray and tan banded wings, wheeled lazily on the high currents. Anna found a sheltered alcove by a brook. As they ate and talked, she became his memory with her mouth tilted up in the corner, her hair brushed behind her left ear, always her left ear, even as it fell across both eyes. He didn't talk much, thinking that tales of his battles or missions in Paris and Vienna would seem out of place.

She was full of stories about Márta. She weighed two

kilos when she was born and Anna had worried. But as a young girl, Márta had shown a fierceness that made up for size. When she was four she took a book from the shelf, shoved it in her mother's hand and commanded, *Read*. She lost none of her fire as she grew. Boys her age, and older, were afraid of her.

Anna became wistful, her eyes half closed. "I didn't have more children. We tried, but the first boy died after six months. The second one, two days after he was born. So, I let Márta have her own way, maybe too often. But she can read, write, herd, and farm."

During a lull in the conversation, Janós stretched out on the ground and closed his eyes, seeing himself with her, raising a daughter. She lay back in the grass.

"I think I'm softer." And guided her on top of him. Ironically, their experiences over the last twenty years made them hesitant with one another the second time. They fumbled with hooks and buttons, kissed and touched tentatively, lifted their heads and looked at one another, giggling at their clumsiness. Though what followed, his need, her warmth and eagerness, frightened him in its intensity, cracking barriers he'd erected around his feelings. In a daze they dressed, mounted their horses and rode back to her cottage. There, he was awkward helping her dismount. He shuffled his feet and stammered. She made it easy. She rose on her toes and kissed him quickly. "I'll see you again."

He mounted Zeno and let the horse wander slowly

back to his tenant's cottage. Katlin was outside waiting for him.

"Jan, is something wrong?"

"Wrong?"

"You're late, and you are flush and look exhausted. What happened?"

"Nothing, nothing. I'm going to turn in early."

* * *

Janós rode out to meet up with his squadrons in the mountains. Five hundred soldiers in peasant clothes. Horses stripped of military accoutrement.

"Every evening you will move out of the mountains. You have your maps. You will be on every path a rebel could use. Find him. Capture him. Return before dawn."

The soldiers trickled out of the mountains into hornbeam and oak covered knolls, behind grassy hillocks, and into the sandy stream beds below Miskolc. The second night, four rebel bands attacked government buildings and the garrison in town. As they returned to their cottages, soldiers sprung from hiding places. Fifty rebels were captured and taken to the stockade in the mountains.

The next night was quiet, the next night, and the next. Janós knew the rebels might think they could hold off until the soldiers got tired of waiting and went back to Buda, but he had prepared for this with extra rations and the promise of extended leave when the campaign ended.

Then, seven rebel attacks. No one was killed, but ten soldiers were wounded and three captured. Seventy rebels were captured. No one would divulge the names of their leaders. There followed two weeks with sporadic small eruptions. János understood the need for patience but circumstances were wearying him. To maintain the fiction he was unaffiliated with the military campaign, he had supper with Katalin and Imre every night and suffered conversations about sheep and cattle diseases. "You know how it is with foot rot," Imre said, "First they go a little lame, then the skin between the claws swells up and the claws separate."

János grimaced as Imre illustrated with a loaf of bread and peppers the depth of the separation and redness of the flesh.

"The fetid smell is worse than skunk," he added.

"I need some fresh air," János said.

* * *

Riding into the plain from the hills, János saw a rider streaking through the fields. Márta, by her speed and streaming hair. He spurred Zeno and angled toward her path. Seeing him, she held up.

"You're looking for a rematch?" She joked.

"No. Something else. I know you didn't want me to talk to the garrison commander, but he's new and served under me in Croatia. A good man, Hungarian."

She spread her hands out in a what's-that-going-to-do gesture.

"He promised to investigate the murder. I know he'll punish the man who shot your father."

She smiled, the first time. "Thank you, Jan, thank you. Oh, I have a question. You said you're not involved with the soldiers around here, but what would you do if you were a rebel, to try to outwit them?"

"That would be a long conversation, and from what I hear, the rebel tactics seem quite effective. They could teach the army."

"I see. By the way, you want a rematch on the race?"

"To the creek."

This time he won, but only by a head. They smiled and rode off in separate directions.

* * *

Janós knocked at Anna's door. It flew open and Márta stormed out, yelling back, "Jan's here," and shoved past him.

"Maybe I should go."

"No, stay. An argument about the harvest." She led him to the small bench, sat close, and took his arm.

"I've been thinking about things, about you, about us," she said. "It's been a very long time, and a lot has happened."

"I've been thinking too." He stood up, very formally went down on one knee and held out his hand. "Anna, will you come back with me to Buda, will you marry me?"

She smiled and lowered her eyes. "Yes, I will."

The door crashed open. Márta stormed in, flushed, and pointed at Jan. "Mother, did you know he is the army commander here? Our neighbors are rotting in a mountain stockade because of him."

Anna stood with a start. Anger added to her height.

"Márta! You cannot come in here and level accusations like that. Apologize."

"I won't." She turned, and slammed the door.

Anna wheeled on János. "Is it true? You're in charge and you haven't told me. After all these years you come to my home. Like a fool, I thought it was because of me."

She backed against the wall, putting as much distance as possible between them.

"Did you think about me? Being seen with an officer in the Austrian army while this was going on. I've told everyone you're the same person I grew up with: someone they can trust."

János took a step toward her. "I'm sorry. I should have said something. I've never forgotten you. That's why I came. Forgive me."

She reached up, put her hands on his shoulders, pushed him down in a chair, and drew another up in front of him. Her eyes were flinty and her mouth a thin white line. "Márta is our daughter, yours and mine."

Janós felt the walls close in, the sun sitting on top of him. He heard the blood moving through his head, racing his thoughts, jumbling his feelings. Anna's face was shrouded in light, distorted. He kneeled and put his arms around her.

"I have missed so much. You, being with you, having a family."

Minutes passed before either of them breathed. Then she took his head in her hands and bent her face to his. "Be careful, be very careful. Our daughter is one of the rebels. You must make absolutely sure nothing happens to her."

"I promise. She will be safe. On my life."

* * *

What was he going to do to protect her? Follow her from the cottage, capture her, and keep her in a safe place? He didn't know. But when he arrived in camp, a delegation of farmers was waiting for him. "Jan, you're a son of the land, you know we should start the harvest now. Look at the clouds, the air is heavy with rain. You have two hundred of our most able men."

"Bring me the leaders of this rebellion and I'll release the men in the stockade."

"But we don't know who they are."

"That surprises me, but I'm confident you'll find out. Come back when you have them."

After the farmers left, Janós spat out orders, "Prepare for an attack on the stockade. Triple the guards. Post men along the mountain paths. Remember, our goal is to capture, not kill. Your rifle is your last weapon, your last."

That evening the rebels were allowed to come up the mountains to the stockade. They fell back in disarray when met by the reinforced guard. Scrambling down dark paths, the rebels were picked up by waiting soldiers. Another hundred were captured. The stockade was jammed.

Within an hour, the delegation of farmers was back with five men in ropes trailing them on foot. In the flicker of the camp fires, Janós saw the rebel leaders ranged from grizzled farmers to young men. He thought he recognized an acquaintance from twenty years ago and turned to avoid eye contact.

"There are no more? You are sure?

"Yes sir, we are sure," the delegation chorused.

"If you are wrong, you will never worry about a harvest again."

Janós stood back, crossed his arms, ordered the men in the stockade released and went into his tent to write his report to Bauer. He'd send the five to Buda. The general would deal with the traitors.

"You promised! You promised!" Shrieking like a diving falcon.

"She tried to escape. I didn't know it was her. No one knew it was her."

"On your life, you said." And hit him hard across the face with her fist. Instinctively, his arm came up. Hurriedly, he dropped it. They looked at Márta, at one another, back, her face tightening, muscles straining to clamp down her terror. His head bowed, mouth drooped open.

Anna dipped a cloth in lavender water and gently wiped Márta's forehead, cheeks, and mouth, kissing her as she did. She handed him the basin. "Throw the water into that pile of rocks at the corner of the field." When he came back she had covered the mirror and extinguished the fire.

"Her eyes, they're sinking into her head. God, help me."

Janós had seen people die many times, but not this way, this close—skin purpling and becoming waxy, hands and feet turning blue. Anna turned the girl on her side to wash her back, now dark purple-black from pooled blood. When she was finished, she placed a white woolen blanket over her. "This will keep her warm," she said, then sat down, put her head in her hands, quietly keening and rocking. He knelt beside the chair, arm around her. For hours, it seemed, his arm numb, not wanting to move it, needing her to feel he shared her grief, not wanting to give into his own despair.

* * *

At daybreak, they moved to the window. They watched the driving rain create black sooty mold spots on the wheat. "Look at me, I'm a shell, empty." She put her face in her hands and sobbed, turned and walked to the door.

"Don't leave."

At the doorway, she turned and faced him.

"We lost a child. We cannot let that destroy us. We should not drown her memory in bitterness," he said.

She closed her eyes and bowed her head.

"Come back to Buda with me. Give us a chance."

He put his hand on her shoulder.

"Please."

Village of St. Fiacre

Michel heard the rooster crow and bounded from bed. *Merde. I should have been home. The sheep, they're supposed to be sheared today.*

His eyes lingered on the downy Thérèse, tousled tawny hair radiant in the morning light. He pulled on his pants and clogs, grabbed his shirt and ran out.

* * *

Gaston opened up the café, looked out, noticed a gangly figure with unkempt ginger hair trying to pull on his shirt as he scampered across the square. Third time in two weeks.

The café had been there fifty years, its blue and glass front a contrast to the stone buildings around it—a crèmerie and a boulangerie. The interior of the café was long and narrow, a zinc bar ran the length of the right wall, tables and chairs, the left. Etched mirrors on both sides lit the room with endless reflections.

The obelisk in the center of the square, once-white, had aged. The plaque at the base of the monument listed forty names under the inscription *Mort pour la France 1914-1918*. Therese's father and Michel's father were listed. In school the two had become close friends against the *you're a bastard, you're a bastard* taunts of their classmates.

* * *

Thérèse woke dreamily, wrapped herself in a blanket and padded across the room to the stove. The cat pressed against her warm ankle.

"Michel is always leaving before I get up," she complained to the cat.

* * *

Gaston, round head crowned with a thatch of snow, munched on a brioche while reading the newspaper. When Thérèse opened the door to the café, he looked up, bright blue eyes magnified by glasses, an expression of glad-you-were-able-to-make-it on his face.

"I didn't think you'd need me early," she said, a pink glow spreading under her olive complexion.

"You'll never guess who I saw running through the square this morning," Gaston winked, "Without a shirt."

She rearranged the cups and glasses she had put away the day before.

* * *

Sunlight streamed through Agnès's window, warming her bedroom. Eyes half open, she turned toward her boys curled up in the corner of the room.

Hearing Agnès stir, her mother announced from the kitchen, "Michel never came home last night."

The smooth sheet on the other side of the bed confirmed the accusation. "Damn," Agnès hissed. "What's he up to?"

"What did you say, dear?"

Agnès knew her mother wouldn't let Michel's absence go with only one comment.

"I told you he was a bastard. He'll never amount to anything. Two children and where is he now?"

"That's not fair. Michel works hard. It's not his fault the sheep got foot rot and we had to move in."

"If you keep having babies we'll have to get a bigger cottage."

* * *

The sun was setting when Michel returned from shearing. He needed a beer, but had a hard time finding a seat in the café. Shepherds and farmers were crowded around the door. Thérèse seemed even more desirable than when he'd left her that morning with tangled hair cascading over bare shoulders and dancing hazel eyes. But she was flirting with the other shepherds.

He stood by the door. Gaston brought him a drink. "You were in a hurry this morning."

"Overslept." Michel took a swig. "But got there on time."

The beer had no taste, but he kept drinking and watching Thérèse. She didn't seem to see him.

* * *

The moon was up before Michel stuck his head in the door of his mother-in-law's cottage.

"Where were you last night?" Agnes asked.

"I fell asleep in the pasture. I woke up in the middle of the night, but stayed away because I didn't want to disturb your mother."

"And this evening?"

"I had to get the sheep settled back in the pasture. You know how skittish they can be after being sheared." Michel shrugged. "And then there was a beer with my friends.":

Her mother injected, "I hope you don't believe the story of *one beer*."

"Mother, please, this is between Michel and me."

* * *

A layer of low fog covered the village and surrounding hills. The sun turned the damp night into a pearly dawn. Thérèse and Gaston were in the café preparing for the morning crush. Michel stopped by for his coffee. Gaston started spouting about the politicians in Paris. Michel nodded absently, drank up and left.

"Your cap." Thérèse ran to catch him.

He continued to walk. She took his arm and lowered her eyes. "I'm sorry about last night, it was so busy."

* * *

Michel was waylaid by his friend Felix on the way out to the pasture. "I need to talk with you about a special girl." He looked down at his clogs, abashed.

"Marie, Suzanne, Colette?"

"I want to get her a small something."

"Girls like things: rings, necklaces, bracelets, you know."

"But I don't have any money."

"Flowers, take her flowers. Look around, they're free. And maybe some chocolate."

* * *

Toward the end of the day, Thérèse told Gaston she needed to go home for a couple of minutes. She'd be back. She'd forgotten to leave milk out for the cat.

"Of course," Gaston smiled. "The cat."

In the square, Thérèse saw the village priest walking towards the café. It wasn't that long ago he'd seemed like a giant. Today he was hardly up to her shoulder.

"My child, may I speak with you?"

A queasy-dampish feeling crept along her arms and down her back. *He knows?*

"What do you want to talk about?"

"A little chat, that's all," and slowly made his way to the café.

* * *

The priest leaned across the bar to whisper to Gaston, "Tell me, my son, is everything alright here?"

"Certainly Father, what's on your mind?" Gaston continued to wipe the counter.

"I don't wish to start rumors, but I've heard things about Thérèse." He raised his bushy brows quizzically.

Gaston shrugged. "Have a drink, Father." and thought that if the 80-year-old priest had gotten wind of her affair with Michel, it had gone on too long.

* * *

"Michel, it's a beautiful ring," Thérèse said. "A perfect fit. What a beautiful surprise."

"I hoped you'd be happy. You'll think of me when you wear it?"

Michel knew she was chagrined because all the other girls had at least one piece of jewelry and she had nothing. More and more he sensed her impatience when he left early, arrived late or missed a rendezvous. He saw the ring in a shop window after getting paid for the wool: *No one knows how much I got paid.*

Thérèse pranced around her cottage, hand held high,

so the garnet refracted the light of the streaming sun, red slivers flashing against the chalk walls.

"I don't know how I can ever thank you," she said and shooed the cat off the bed.

"And I've been thinking of how you would," and took the cat's place.

* * *

On Saturday evening, everyone in town attended the dance in the square. Thérèse and her friend Marie stood in front of the café.

"Thérèse, isn't that Felix?" Marie asked. "By the obelisk."

Thérèse shrugged.

"I thought you liked him."

"Those light blue eyes, dark hair, that smile, and those arms. Imagine them around you." Thérèse shivered as she spoke.

"I'm imagining," Marie said, "Why don't you go over? Maybe he'll ask you to dance."

"What's the use? He's so poor his clothes are rags. I'd be surprised if his whole family has ten sheep."

* * *

A small band set up on the steps of the town hall. At the first sound of the music for the bourrée, Michel took Agnès's hand and joined three other couples. They whirled and twirled, mindless of children and her mother as they spun. The music ended and they collapsed in laughter in one another's arms.

This was how Michel remembered the life they had before they moved in with her mother. Since, it had been: *Not now, she might hear.*

* * *

Next day, Michel broke away from the family gathering. He told Agnès he needed to go out to check on the sheep. A couple of them looked as if they were developing scrapie.

Thérèse was there, pouting in a grove of oak trees at the edge of the pasture.

"What are you doing out here in the open? From the road, anyone could see."

"Where have you been? I've been here for hours."

"Dinner went on and on. You know how her mother is."

Michel reached for her hand. "I see you're wearing your grandmother's ring."

Thérèse raised herself on tip toe and gave him a long warm kiss.

"Thank you so much, Grand-mama."

* * *

Agnès's mother was buying her morning bread when the baker's wife came from behind the counter.

"Madame, you know I am not a gossip, but when I see something like I saw yesterday."

She nodded.

"I was coming back from a visit to my sister, you know she lives along the road outside of town. I saw something moving in that grove of oak trees in the pasture. You know the one. From the road it looked like young children, so I thought I should check. One can't be too careful about children these days."

She took a deep breath and wiped her lips with a handkerchief. "All I can say is that it was Michel and Thérèse. That's all I can say."

* * *

Gaston looked out on the square and noticed Agnès's mother crabbing toward the town hall. He slid off his stool and walked out to her. They huddled in the shadow of the church steeple.

"Madame, a word. There is a situation. Together, I thought we might…"

* * *

A light knock on Thérèse's door. She opened to see Agnès's mother hunched over in her black dress and shawl. The woman tilted her head to the side and looked up at her with a glinting eye.

"I've come to talk about Michel."

"Why talk to me?"

The woman pushed her way in and sat in the chair by the hearth.

"I don't want my daughter hurt. Michel's a bastard, but he's her bastard and the father of my grandsons."

She waited for a confirming nod from Thérèse, then continued, "There is perhaps an arrangement a young girl like you would find advantageous."

Thérèse looked vacantly around the room, went to the window, tugged at the curtain, took her time looking at people passing in the street.

"I'm not sure." She went over to the bed, picked up the cat and caressed it slowly.

* * *

Michel walked into the café. Thérèse was laughing with Gaston and Marie.

"Have you heard?" Gaston cried. "Thérèse asked me to be the father of the bride."

Michel froze, looked at Thérèse who was miming *I meant to tell you.* He forced out a congratulatory, "I'm sure you'll be happy."

"Champagne for everyone." Gaston raised a bottle from behind the bar.

"I just remembered, I left something at home," Michel said.

He turned and bumped into Felix coming in the door. "So you've heard the good news?" In a whisper, "I think it was the chocolate."

Michel continued out the door.

"And you'll be my best man, won't you?" Felix called after him.

Michel took a few steps, stopped, encased in the stifling town square. He watched a small red and black beetle crawl over pebbles between the cobblestones, crossing from the sunlight into the shadow cast by the church steeple.

Slashing at the Nets

She left. After fourteen years.

That morning he'd caught rougets and after he cleaned them, she put them on the grill. The delicate bones were now piled on the plates and his knife lay beside the discarded napkins. They were sipping the last of a bottle of rosé, half dozing side-by-side in weathered chairs on the small balcony. The heat was blistering, unseasonal, bleaching the sky of color. Cats and dogs lay prostrate on the cobblestone streets, stunned into submission, their legs splayed.

A crate load of barrels clattered abruptly and nosily below them. They stood and looked over the balcony. A gray dappled horse, without livery or rider, burst down the narrow street. It veered to the left, skidded, and fell against a stone wall. A raw scream rose from its throat. The horse tried to raise itself, but couldn't, bone protruded from its front leg. It lifted its head to the sky, long yellow teeth jutting from curled lips. Panicked high-pitched whinnies pierced the comatose day. Again and again the animal tried to get up, thrashed and fell down on itself.

"Do something." She grabbed his arm and shook him. "Put it out of its misery." The veins in her neck stood out.

"How? I don't have a gun."

She grabbed his knife, ran out of the house, slowed as she approached the horse, to not frighten him. Soft gentle words dropped to a low cooing sound. The horse calmed. She placed his head in her lap, laid her hand over his wild eye, put her mouth to his ear and slit his jugular.

The animal shuddered. She pressed her cheek to his neck and watched his blood empty into the street.

Rising, black hair matted against her frozen bloodied face, she walked back into the house, her dress now carmine.

"How?" She brushed past him. "That's how," and slumped in a corner of the room, tears blotching her cheeks. He stood statue-like, staring.

She waved the knife at him. "Did someone use this to cut off your balls? What's happened to you? Last month, those boys in the orchard that threw oranges at us, the man who stole fish from your friend in the market: you ran away. Now this."

The knife she'd used on the horse was given to him by his father when he was ten, his first year on the boat. When he was twelve, his father was swept out to sea, his body never found. The knife was his inheritance. Then, the horn handle was pale yellow and striated, the blade was thick and blue-black. Now, the grip was dark and smooth and the blade had been honed silver.

He used the same knife to defend her years earlier. On a nearby island. They'd met in a bar. She was standing in the midst of a group of girls. Blue eyes, the genetic gift of a visiting Englishman three generations earlier. That's what set her apart. When the band played, her lithe body swayed as if the music were coming up marrow deep.

Later that week, they walked hand-in-hand along a dark path at the edge of town. Four men came out of the trees, surrounded them, taunted them: island slut, mainland bastard. Knives were drawn. He replied with daring. The four fled, but not before leaving a long slash on his left arm.

She came back to the mainland with him. And for all the years they were together she massaged ointments into his scar every night. She was shining a medal of honor.

It was last year, in a rain storm, he'd asked a friend to help on the boat. They reached the fishing grounds, half a mile off-shore and set the nets when lightning crackled and the wind kicked up. A rogue wave knocked his friend into the sea. The friend struggled and became tangled in the nets. He dove in, slashed at the nets, again and again, but the seines would not release their grip. His knife failed him. His friend drowned. He was responsible. Since, each time thunder cracks the sky, it is his friend's last wail. Fear washes over him, robs him of certainty.

After she'd gone that day, he went down to the shore and took a bottle with him. For company. For who the hell knows what. Hours later he fell into a deep sleep.

In the morning, a salty mist coated his face, even his eyelids. Circling gulls brayed overhead. He pulled himself out of the sand and settled against an overturned rowboat.

Down the beach, he noticed a crab working its way out of the water. It skittered up the sand, then was pulled back by the surf. It sidled up again and succeeded in outrunning the chasing waves. The crab paused, exhausted by its struggle, only to be snatched up by a goddamn gull.

He yanked himself up from the sand and hurled his knife. Gull, crab, and knife plummeted to the rocks, spouting forth a spray of steel shards, shell fragments, and white feathers.

The Thief and the Baby

The robbery didn't go right. She was supposed to be shopping. She came back just as he found the money.

The next morning, Fausto woke up tired. He'd replayed the scene over and over that night, watching the movie loop on the ceiling. Slowly he climbed into his coveralls and went into the kitchen, finding some bread and cherry jam his wife had left for him. After a few bites, he picked up his toolbox and headed out for coffee. An hour later than usual, but he thought his friends might still be at the café. On the way, he passed a news kiosk. A huge headline in *La Repubblica.*

APARTMENT ROBBERY
WOMAN LOSES BABY

Robbery. Apartment. The bitter after-taste of cherries choked him. He dug into his pocket for ninety centisimi to buy the paper. The coins spilled on the sidewalk, between the cobblestones and into the street. He scuttled on his hands and knees. Reaching under a parked car, he scraped the top of his hand. Merda. He hurried into a caffè where he wasn't known. A narrow place, bits of paper and butts littered the floor, cigarette smoke and stale beer haze. The kind of café that survived on the small band of pensioners holding on to the bar. He ordered an espresso and stared at the paper, willing himself to focus.

Casatenovo (Lecco) 18 May. She lost her baby. Her first, he was due in two weeks. According to the grieving mother-to-be, Maria Patrizio Magni, 29, a thief ran out of her apartment on Via della Misericordia yesterday, hit her and she fell down the stairs.

"He slammed into me, knocked me hard, just as I came in the door," she said from her hospital bed.

The baby's grandfather discovered the tragedy. Maria Patrizio bleeding and semi-conscious, lying at the bottom of the stairs.

In addition to the tragic death, four hundred euros the family saved for the birth and baptism celebrations were missing.

In a statement last evening, Il colonnello Luciano Garofano vowed, "The carabinieri will hunt down the heartless thief who grievously harmed a mother and killed her baby, a vile act. The killer will be found."

Killer! Fausto's skin felt hot, tiny prickling fires pocked his face and neck, sweat chilled his back. His hand jerked and hit his cup. Half the coffee ran off the table onto his pants. *I didn't kill anyone, I only took some money.* The barista came over to help. He mumbled something, got up, knocked the chair over and left. He staggered into a small piazza surrounded by flaking yellow buildings with sagging shutters and broken tile roofs. Lines of wet laundry and hanging pots of geraniums competed for sunlight. He slipped, caught himself, stumbled, ended up slumped against the base of a graffiti laced fountain. Mothers, toddlers in tow, veered away in disgust at the sight of his stained pant leg. *What if the police find me? What would happen to my boys?* Eventually, he smelled the piss a mongrel dog had sprayed earlier, and got up.

He forced himself to walk the few blocks back to his van, but flooded the engine twice before it started. The street signs made no sense, twice he took a wrong turn. *Killer!* Outside town, he drove south on SP 51, stopped on the shoulder of the road and walked into the woods. When he was a boy, he'd often gone into the forest that bordered his step-father's farm. It had been the place to get away from his quarreling family. The scent of resin and the quiet of the pine needle floor calmed him, allowed him to think.

Yesterday, he spent 50 euros from the robbery on roses for Giulia and treats for his boys, Alessandro and Matteo. He loved being able to bring his family surprises.

This way he knew he was taking care of them. Increasingly difficult since the economy slumped and work for carpenters disappeared.

He sat down against a pine tree, trying to figure out what happened. Every job was planned to the last detail. He spent days watching people go in and out, and mapping escape routes. For three years, his robberies had gone off without a problem. Until yesterday, when she walked into the apartment. He remembered a tight pink skirt and a red lace blouse. Thin face.

I'm not a killer, he kept repeating. The woman always left early, she wasn't supposed to be there. *I just brushed her shoulder when I ran by. Not enough to make her fall.*

* * *

The next morning, he went to Cippa's for coffee with his friends Claudio and Silvio. On the way, it seemed like the people he passed were eyeing him, knew what he'd done. By the time he reached the caffè, his shirt was wet with perspiration.

Caffè Cippa was chrome and glass, pastry and gelato cases in front and a gleaming red espresso maker behind the bar. A freshly ground coffee scent strong enough to drink. No trouble spotting the pair in the back: Claudio with heavy gold chains, shiny purple shirt and shoulder length hair, Silvio in his Milano AC shirt, (broad black and red vertical stripes), and bulging blue eyes. They were performing their morning ritual: Silvio shouted and waved his arms and Claudio pretended to listen.

"Hey, Fausto," Silvio called. "You missed all the excitement yesterday."

"Yeah, imagine stealing a couple hundred euros and ending up with a dead baby on your hands?" Claudio pulled his chains up like a noose. "I bet that guy doesn't try to pull a job again."

A wave of nausea poured over Fausto. He flopped down in a chair.

"But did you see the picture of the mother," Silvio said. "A babe, pretty, brown eyes, blonde. Paper says she danced on a game show, too bad they didn't give us a full length shot."

"Do you read the paper or gawk at pictures?" Claudio asked. "She's in the hospital, staring at the wall, poor kid."

"Fausto, you're out of it this morning. What's your take?"

"How about Leonardo last night? That header over the goalie."

"We're talking about a dead baby, not a football match, idiot."

They looked at one another, twisted mouths, raised eyebrows, shrugged, and took another sip of coffee.

* * *

I did think about her coming back early. It was all planned. I'd hide behind a chair or sofa, then sneak out. It had all started so easily. The first key on his ring of masters opened the door. From the looks of the living room she was gone for a while. Everything in place. Magazines stacked in neat piles. Baby clothes sorted on a table in the bedroom. He searched the large chest in the living room, checked the dresser in the bedroom, found the money under towels in the kitchen. That's where he was when heard the front door open. Desperation messed with his judgment. He had resorted to a money lender to pay last month's rent and the loan was due. The guy told him that if he didn't pay on time he'd end up with a busted leg.

"Ask Guido over on via Garibaldi, if ya don't believe me. Yeah, and I know where your son Alessandro goes to school." Fausto almost backed out of the deal when he heard that, *but what could I do?*

* * *

He paid off the money lender, then drove to via Leone, a street where doctors and lawyers lived. This month's rent was now ten days overdue. He needed to pull another job quickly, and carefully. He needed to think, pull this cold vise off his head. He'd spent a little time on this street last week selecting likely targets, but didn't have time for his usual planning. The apartment buildings were new but designed to replicate the style of Roman villas: red masonry, black columns, mosaics. He parked across from number 32 and sat in his small gray Fiat van, the type made for Lilliputian tradesmen. Mid-afternoon, he took his toolbox from the cargo area and went inside. The large front door opened onto a tiled courtyard. Stone planters with box wood shrubs surrounded a small fountain. Some of his anxiety faded in surroundings where a carpenter and his tools were accepted sights. And physically, Fausto did not attract attention: 5'7", slight build, shaggy black hair and a rather long nose that turned right as it left his face. He scanned the names on the mailboxes, found a doctor, second floor on the right. He rang the bell, no one answered, and rang again. He walked upstairs, looked at the lock. *I've got a key for this one.* Back in the van, he continued watching. No one came out of the building. At six, residents started to trickle in. At eight, a couple carrying bundles entered the building, two minutes later there were lights in the doctor's apartment. Afternoon would be the time to pull the job.

Giulia was standing in the door when he got home, her long black hair pulled back against her head. Though 4' 10" and petite, she bored into Fausto's eyes with a ferocity that made him wince.

"And where have you been?"

He shrugged. "On a job, why?"

"No one was there."

"The contractor had an emergency repair on the other side of town."

"And you couldn't let me know? The one day I needed your help. Matteo's in the hospital."

Behind her at the kitchen table, his older son Alessandro had stopped eating his supper. His eyes were glued on his mother scolding his father.

"What happened?"

"The same thing that happens to all boys who jump out of trees, a concussion and a broken leg. No one knew where you were, and Matteo kept asking for you."

She poked him in the chest. "Now go see him."

The acrid tang of disinfectant hit Fausto when he walked into the hospital. The information desk was empty so he wandered up and down long vacant corridors until he found Matteo. Groggy from the pain pills, his mud brown hair was matted across his face and his usual wide eyes were barely slits. His sheets were in a tangle, like he'd had bad dreams and thrashed around in his sleep. Fausto put his hand on Matteo's shoulder and whispered, "I'm here now." The boy didn't move.

I'm a nothing. A baby died. The police are after me. Giulia is mad. Matteo is a mess. He turned and shuffled out of the room and down the stairs to his van. He didn't want to go home, so stopped at a bar. Everyone was eyelocked into the TV, he sat at the far end of the counter and ordered a whiskey. It went down quickly and he ordered another. The game show, *l'eredita*, came on, with girls dancing around the MC. According to the papers, the baby's mother, Maria Patrizio, had performed on a show like this.

He got back to the apartment after eleven. Giulia was asleep. When he tried to sleep, a baby's face fused with Matteo's face, became Matteo, Matteo sprawled on the ground, Mirko in Matteo's bed. Fausto and Maria Patrizio. Saucer eyes and gaping mouth. She was at the bottom of the stairs, blood streaming from her body.

* * *

He woke up, couldn't get his eyes to open and stumbled into the kitchen. Giulia was drinking her coffee, flipping through *Donna Moderna*.

"Pick Matteo up from the hospital at noon."

Giulia went back to her magazine. He knew she could smell his fear. Her eyes were unblinking, her lips a pencil line, her voice low and calm. "Why did you lie to me yesterday?"

"I got it all mixed up—the address, the job, everything. I was working with Claudio."

"Funny, Claudio's wife came into the shop yesterday morning. She said they were leaving for her mother's on the noon train."

"I don't know what to say."

"How about the truth? Where were you? What were you doing? What are you hiding?"

Her questions were bullets aimed at his head. How he imagined the police would be when they picked him up.

"You've been acting strangely the last couple days. There's something you're not telling me."

Her eyes were troubled and her forehead as wrinkled as her mother's.

* * *

Despite the pretty nurses hovering over him, his son acted bruised when Fausto picked him up. He was too, after he paid the two-hundred euro hospital bill. He was determined to make it up to Matteo for not being there after he fell, so on the ride home did his imitations of Pinocchio, Il Duce, Il Papa (with his German accent) and topped off with Pulcinella. The character's high-pitched peep, like a frightened chick, put Matteo into a spasm of giggles. Fausto carried him up to their apartment, laid him in Giulia's arms and left.

He drove over to via Leone and sat outside at a caffè. It rested in a collection of small shops: bakery, dress store, pharmacy, and a hair salon. Fausto liked to sit and watch, gauge the rhythm of the traffic around his targets. Still, he was anxious because he had spent so little time casing the apartment, that, and the owner of the café came out on the sidewalk three or four times, looked around at the other patrons, but when his eyes shifted to Fausto, they narrowed and lingered. *Had Maria Patrizio described me?* Fausto left before he was ready. He knew if he didn't act now, he'd never pull another job.

He rang the bell of the doctor's apartment. No one answered, went up two flights of stairs, tried the door, locked. He took a ring of master keys from his pocket, the second one worked. The salon was paneled in dark wood, furnished with tapestries, oriental carpets, silver bowls, and candlesticks. A grandfather clock ticked loudly on the far wall. This job was going well, he'd have time to look around, find the best stuff. He knew where he could get a good price for silver and he was sure he'd find money in a drawer, every Italian's second bank.

A woman's voice from the inside of the apartment called, "Angelo, is that you?"

Damn. He turned, caught his heel on the rug, missed the first step out the door, recovered his balance, but slipped on the top stair. His toolbox fell. Its latch popped open and as he tumbled down the stairs, hammer, screwdriver, and chisels rained down on him. He lay at the bottom long enough to feel every sprain and bruise, wrenched himself up, gathered the tools and stumbled out of the building. Only then did he notice his head and hands were bleeding.

He cleaned himself up and drove home, mumbled

something to Giulia about falling down. She washed and put iodine and bandages on his cuts and tucked him in bed with a tisane. When he tried to get out of bed next morning, he couldn't.

Back asleep, stairs, falling, hammers raining down, blood, blood gushing. Babies thrashing. He would save them, but couldn't get close. He had to keep on. They faded from sight. One step more. Then he fell, down a long stairway, into darkness, no longer breathing. He screamed himself awake.

Giulia looked in on him when she got back. "What's wrong? You look like you've seen a ghost."

Iron bands were being pulled across his chest. They became tighter and tighter, he inhaled, couldn't exhale, couldn't swallow, couldn't breathe, opened his eyes, the room was black and spinning in front of him. He shook himself, bolted upright and shrieked. Giulia ran in, saw his convulsed face and called 118.

* * *

The hospital room was bare. One chair and a large crucifix, black wood and a twisted Christ figure. Fausto heard murmurs and saw a tall gangly man in a long white coat hunched like a stork over Giulia. He heard bits of their conversation, "Brain scans…no physical damage… emotional trauma…a death? His mother? A baby?"

When the doctor left, Giulia pulled a chair up to her husband's bed: her eyes bruised and sunken into her small face, her arms wrapped tightly around her body. Fausto had never seen her so frightened.

"Baby." He reached out from under the covers, took her wrist, and pulled her closer. He whispered, "Lost baby."

She leaned down. "What are you talking about?"

"I was the thief. Three years. No other way to get money."

"Stealing for three years? Did you think of the boys, of me? What this would do to us? Madonna, help me."

She turned away and bent down in the chair, face on her knees. She gasped for air and shook. A hush, as her body gathered itself.

"I didn't know what else to do. I did it for you and the boys."

She swung around, jerked his face to hers, and hissed, "Listen, you stupid bastard, don't say a word to anyone. Tomorrow we'll figure out what to do."

At the door, she turned back toward him. "Idiot."

* * *

A week later, Giulia brought Fausto home accompanied by a small satchel of pills. They went into the bedroom while he unpacked his clothes. When he finished, they stood awkwardly on opposite sides of the bed.

"Sit down and listen. Find a job, a real job, and find it now. You will spend every waking moment looking until you get one, you understand."

That evening Giulia and the boys tried to make supper a special event for his first night home. Alessandro showed him how he kicked the winning goal at the last game and Matteo did <u>his</u> imitation of Pulcinella, but nothing seemed to pierce Fausto's haze. The boys went off to play video games.

* * *

Every day he bought the paper to look at the help wanted ads. Nothing. He drove to every building site in Casatenovo and the surrounding area. Nothing. And every time he got in and out of his van, his body reminded him of his fall. And for a month every evening after supper he had to tell Giulia, Nothing. But, after dinner one night he announced. "I've got a lead. A new factory is going up south of town, and they're looking for people to do the framing."

While Giulia put the boys to bed, he looked through

drawers in the living room. He found the one where they kept their documents: birth certificates, marriage license. She came in and asked him what he was doing. He shoved the life insurance policy back into the drawer and told her he was looking for his carpenter's certificate.

"They'll want that for the job tomorrow."

Fausto got up early and put on his overalls. He kissed Giulia on the cheek and was rewarded with a sleepy smile. He went into the other bedroom with its warm-slumber aroma of boys tangled in their covers. He walked out of the apartment and down the steps to his van. He drove south on SP 51. Outside of town, he stopped on the shoulder of the road by the woods, lifted the hood and tied a white rag on the antenna. He stood by the van drinking in the wet morning fog. In the clearing, boys were playing soccer. He felt the breeze of cars whizzing by and heard the wail of an approaching truck.

Acknowledgements

The stories in this collection have been shaped by many talented teachers and writing colleagues. The stories are better told for their care and craft. Thank you Rae Bryant, Janet Freeman, Ivy Hansen, Suzanne Rivecca, Benjamin Percy, Jess Walter, Nancy Packer, M.M. DeVoe, Alexis Santi, Kay Sexton, Skip Horack, Eric Puchner, Beverly Jackson, Peter Biello, Marko Fong, Cezarija Abartis, Judith Beck, Lisa K. Clark, Lucinda Nelson Dhavan, Bernice Fisher, Jeff Rose, and Marie Shield. And thank you Adrienne Brodeur and Jamie Kravitz for creating a convivial and creative atmosphere at Aspen Summer Words. Five of the stories in this collection benefitted from workshops at Aspen.

Earlier versions of the stories have appeared in *Bartleby Snopes*, *Crimson Highway*, *Danse Macabre*, *Forge*, *Dark Sky Magazine*, *Grey Sparrow Journal*, *Lacuna*, *Muscadine Lines*, *Neonbeam*, *Next to the Knuckle*, *Pine Tree Mysteries*, *Our Stories*, and *The Linnet's Wings*. Thank you editors, for your support and encouragement.

Thank you Jan, Bob, and Mark Babcock, Ashley Clarke, and Matt King, the lovely people at Deeds Publishing, for appreciating these tales and bringing them to readers in a stylish and elegant fashion.

To my first, best, and last reader who, more than anyone, provided encouragement, inspiration, fabulous editing, and great story lines: thank you Beverly Mills.

About the Author

Townsend Walker grew up in western Maryland and graduated from Georgetown (B.S. Foreign Service), New York University (M.A. Economics), and Stanford (Ph.D. Economics).

During a career in banking, he lived in New York, Paris, London, Rome, and San Francisco and wrote three books on finance: *A Guide for Using the Foreign Exchange Market, Managing Risk with Derivatives,* and *Managing Lease Portfolios.*

His ideas come from cemeteries, foreign places, paintings, violence, and strong women. His novella, *La Ronde,* was published by Truth Serum Press in 2015. His stories have appeared in over seventy literary journals and have been included in ten anthologies. "A Little Love, A Little Shove" and "Holding Tight" were nominated for a PEN/O. Henry Award. Four stories were performed at the New Short Fiction Series in Hollywood.

Townsend currently lives in San Francisco and in addition to working on his stories, he teaches a workshop in creative writing to incarcerated veterans at San Quentin State Prison.

Visit Townsend online at www.townsendwalker.com

CPSIA information can be obtained
at www.ICGtesting.com
Printed in the USA
LVHW091731090119
603304LV00003B/563/P